# The Other Place

# Dawn Knox

British Library Cataloguing in Publication Data A Record of this Publication is available from the British Library

ISBN: 9798839521766

Formatting and Cover © Paul Burridge at www.publishingbuddy.co.uk
Editing – Wendy Ogilvie Editorial Services

To my mum, Amelia May, after whom I named the ship, the Lady Amelia. And to my dad.

Thank you both for believing in me.

# CHAPTER ONE

1790:

Cold porridge, cabbage and lye. Those were the smells that lingered in the dingy passage leading to the workhouse kitchen. But eight-year-old Henry Bonner wasn't gritting his teeth because of the stench – he was used to that – rather, he was putting the utmost concentration into creeping silently along the hall, his shoulder pressed against the cold wall in an attempt to keep to the shadows. He had no business being there and if he was found, he'd be in trouble. Nevertheless, he tiptoed stealthily towards the kitchen door which was slightly ajar.

A rat scuttled out of one of the storerooms and scurried ahead of him to the far end of the passage, making him gasp with fear. He froze, his heart thumping as he waited to see if the noise had alerted anyone. But Mrs Clegg's voice coming from the kitchen didn't falter nor change pitch as she harangued Henry's sister, Keziah. Mrs Clegg, the workhouse master's wife, urged the girl to scrub the floor harder between listing her many shortcomings.

Henry felt a rush of love for his elder sister, tinged with annoyance. If only she'd try not to antagonise the parish officials. Hadn't he warned her... begged her...?

Then, at the tap, tap, tap on the stairs behind him, Henry experienced such a jolt of fear, he thought his heart would stop.

*Run!*

But he knew he'd be seen before he reached the end of the passage.

*Hide!*

Where? The storeroom?

*No! Never!*

He'd been locked in there before as a punishment and at the memory of the stifling darkness, beads of sweat stood out on his brow and his hands pressed against his chest to steady his thrashing heart.

Surely it was better to briefly hide in the tiny, windowless room than to risk being caught and then locked in the darkness for hours...

But it was too late, a woman had arrived at the bottom of the stairs and as she caught sight of Henry, she cocked her head to one side like a puzzled bird. Through tear-filled eyes, Henry saw her wag her finger at him, then to his relief, she placed it over her lips; a signal to remain silent.

Henry slowly exhaled. It was Martha Carter, one of the workhouse nurses who'd taken a liking to Henry and thirteen-year-old Keziah. She wouldn't give him away – although you could never tell with adults – especially not those who worked in the St Margaret's Parish Workhouse. Most of them were more interested in recognition in the parish than doing good works. Henry and Keziah had lived in the workhouse for three years and during that time, they'd been constantly reminded how fortunate pauper children were to receive charity despite placing such a burden on parish funds. Those three years had been desperately unhappy, not least because they'd been separated – Keziah living in the women's half of the building and Henry in the men's. But Martha had always been kind to the Bonner children – well, so far.

Helplessness and hopelessness bore down on him and he clenched his jaw and fists at the injustice of their lives. Until he and Keziah could support themselves, they had no choice but to remain in the workhouse and abide by the harsh rules. They both knew the alternative – living on the street – was not an option. Gangs of ruthless men preyed on orphans, pressing them into begging – or worse – and he and his sister had already glimpsed the disreputable side of London life... Henry shook his head to banish the memory.

"No!" Mrs Clegg screeched from the kitchen, "Do that part again, Keziah Bonner!"

Although a large woman, Martha was light on her feet and she reached Henry quickly, taking him by the shoulders.

What are you doing here? she mouthed. And he knew from her anxious expression, that the tight grip on his shoulders was borne out of concern and frustration at his foolishness in being there – not anger.

Kezzie! he mouthed back.

I should have known, her expression said, and she shook her head reproachfully. The scrape of metal against stone drew Martha's attention away from the boy towards the kitchen door and for a moment her eyes narrowed as if she expected Mrs Clegg to appear and the recriminations to begin. Henry knew it would be difficult for Martha to explain why she was now kneeling in front of him, her hands on his shoulders instead of dragging him back upstairs by the ear. As if arriving at a decision, Martha struggled to her feet and taking Henry by the hand, she pulled him towards the storeroom.

At first, he tried to wrench his hand from hers. Surely she didn't intend to lock him in the dark? But that didn't make sense. If Martha wanted to get him into trouble, she'd only have to call out and Mrs Clegg would have been very happy to oblige.

"Come!" Martha whispered urgently, and there was something in her expression Henry thought he could trust, so he followed her. She opened

2

the door wide to throw a little light into the interior of the storeroom and stepping inside, she lifted folded sheets off a shelf. Giving Henry a small pile, she took the rest herself. It was just as well she'd taken this precaution because Mrs Clegg appeared soundlessly in the passage behind them.

"Young Master Bonner's been helpin' me," Martha said quickly before Mrs Clegg could speak. "What a well-behaved lad he is. A credit to the workhouse, I'd say."

"Indeed." Mrs Clegg seemed slightly bemused as she weighed the situation up. "Good, good," she said finally and then added, "heaven knows, they're like chalk and cheese!" She rolled her eyes to the ceiling and jerked her head towards Keziah who was standing behind her.

Henry knew exactly what she meant. How often had the parish officers used that phrase – usually with an irritated click of the tongue – when referring to Keziah and Henry Bonner?

It wasn't true. Henry knew there were more similarities between them than differences with their snub noses and large eyes, fringed with thick, dark lashes. Both their heads were closely-cropped, like all the other children in the workhouse to keep down the lice, but several years ago, they'd both had long, dark curls.

No, it wasn't their looks Mrs Clegg had referred to as chalk and cheese, it was their personalities. 'Insolent' and 'disobedient' were words Henry often heard associated with 'that Bonner girl' whereas there were few descriptions linked to his name. He'd been told he was a boy who conducted himself in the manner one would expect of a workhouse child.

"Good, good," Mrs Clegg said again to Martha, then turning to Keziah, she snapped, "Well, make haste, girl! Stop your dawdling!"

Before Keziah followed the master's wife up the stairs, she looked at Henry and raised her eyebrows in a silent question, using their secret code. He replied by touching the tip of his nose as if scratching it to let her know he was well, then raised his eyebrows. When she touched the tip of her nose to signal to him she was well, he saw her grazed knuckles, fresh with blood, and guessed she must have slipped while scrubbing the floor. It was just like Keziah to use their private sign language to tell him all was well, when it obviously wasn't. But neither of them ever used the signal that all was not well – scratching the right earlobe – because neither wanted to worry the other and anyway, what could either of them have done about it?

The punishment had been Keziah's fault in the first place. It had been her wish to communicate with Henry that had resulted in her being ordered to scrub the kitchen floor.

Usually, Keziah would initiate this silent eyebrow-raising, nose-scratching conversation during a meal when such gestures would go unnoticed. However, the previous day, she'd been kept apart from the others for some misdemeanour and only allowed dried bread in the kitchen rather than eating Sunday dinner with the others and therefore hadn't seen Henry at all. After the meal, she'd been admitted to the dining hall so she could listen to Mr Welch, the churchwarden, read from the Bible, and in desperation, she'd tried to make contact with Henry but her upturned face amongst so many lowered ones, had been obvious.

Henry, whose eyes had also been downcast, had not looked up until outrage had strangled Mr Welch's droning voice, raising it an octave, as he reprimanded Keziah. Henry had been appalled she'd put herself in the way of more punishment because she'd wanted to find out if he was well. And that, in turn, had prompted, Henry's current, ill-fated attempt to find out if she was well.

Their lives would be so much easier if only Keziah wasn't so foolish and stubborn. She knew the officials were always waiting for an excuse to pounce on her for poor behaviour or showing disrespect, yet she wouldn't do as Henry begged and simply pretend to be good. He had no more love for the people who ran the workhouse than his sister but he knew it made sense to fool them into believing he did. That made him a coward, he knew, yet it also meant his life was easier than Keziah's because she constantly created trouble for herself. And yet, the truth was, if Keziah suffered, so did he.

Henry turned to follow them up the stairs but Martha laid a restraining hand on his shoulder, "Not yet, lad," she said, "let the lass go. It's for the best. I'll tend her grazes later, never you fear, and I'll tell her you came to make sure she was well. But it's best if you keep out of trouble now."

He knew from other warnings that although Martha had said 'now', she meant in the future. She feared he would follow Keziah's example with her defiant glare and even, occasionally, her insolent replies when she was reprimanded. In truth, how he'd have loved to follow her example but he dared not – the incident that still haunted his nightmares would see to that. It had occurred shortly after the Bonner children had arrived at St Margaret's when one of the older boys had insulted his sister and Henry had punched him on the nose. Mr Clegg had told him he wouldn't tolerate violence in his workhouse and that Henry wouldn't, therefore, receive a beating. However, the children in his care needed to understand that anyone who transgressed would be

4

disciplined. Then he'd led the unwary boy down the stairs and thrown him in one of the storerooms where he remained without food or water for the rest of the day.

Five-year-old Henry had never been on his own for long – especially in the darkness and his sobs had subsided to gasps for air. Time had ceased to exist and he'd given up ever seeing light again when Mrs Clegg had opened the door and led him by his ear to his bed. Since then, he'd behaved impeccably and had begged Keziah to do likewise, but she always thought she knew best.

Martha squeezed his shoulder bringing him back from his reverie. "Go now, lad," she said, relieving him of the pile of sheets and nodding towards the stairs. "And don't dillydally!" She winked at him and added, "I'll make sure Keziah is well and has a bite to eat so don't you fret."

Henry swallowed the lump in his throat and somehow managed to mumble, "Thank you, ma'am," before hurrying to the bottom of the stairs. He looked up to check they were empty and raced upwards and away towards the east wing where the men lived, the image of Keziah's grazed knuckles and sad expression still vivid in his mind.

But if Henry longed for his sister to become more prudent, there was plenty about her personality he admired and didn't want her to change – she was loyal, loving and honest. And braver than anyone else he knew. He felt those traits nestled deep inside him too but he had very little opportunity to exercise them. There was no one in his life, other than his sister, who was worth loving, nor who deserved his loyalty and honesty. His bravery was only tested when he risked being caught on the nights he crept out of his dormitory to see her but it was worth it, because, without their meetings, as infrequent as they were, he had no anchor in his life. She was his touchstone and the only link with the past that he found increasingly hard to remember. Without Keziah, what would be the point of living? They were kindred spirits and one thing that bound them together forever was their guilt. Not for the same event, it was true, but Henry knew he had been the cause of their family's troubles and without him, Keziah would not have her bitter regrets.

Keziah winced as Martha bathed her scraped knuckles, then later allowed herself to be encircled in the nurse's strong arms.

"Too troublesome for yer own good," Martha said stroking Keziah's shorn head, "but don't you fret, I'll let young Henry know you're well. He shan't go to bed a-worryin'."

Keziah's eyes stung with hot, bitter tears as she clung to Martha, burying her face against her pillow-like bosom.

The vigorous scrubbing had allowed her to work off the anger she felt towards Mr Welch, the churchwarden. It was he who'd noticed her staring at the men's tables when he'd been reading from the Scripture the previous day. He'd accused Keziah of being brazen-faced as well as disrespectful to God. She knew neither were true but perhaps Henry was right when he told her to show more restraint. After all, everyone loved Henry for his sunny nature although she knew him well enough to realise they didn't see beneath the mask he wished to show them. She often marvelled that a child so young, could behave with such maturity. Certainly, more wisdom than she often showed. But then in his short life, he hadn't seen as much injustice as she had. Nevertheless, had she not behaved so foolishly when she'd been his age, their lives would likely have been quite different. True, she and Henry would probably still be in the workhouse, but they would be accompanied by their elder sister, Eva, who would be sixteen now. If, please God, she was still alive...

It wasn't only Henry who pleaded with Keziah to show more respect even if she didn't feel it. Mr Dawley, the schoolteacher in the charity school had begged her to be more prudent. He'd been impressed with Keziah's reading and arithmetic, and he'd taken special pains with her.

It was his kindness and the occasional soft embrace of the nurse, Martha Carter, that allowed Keziah to believe there was such a thing as the love that was constantly referred to by Mr Clegg and his parish officials. Of course, she loved Henry and knew Henry loved her but since their parents had died, the world had been a dark, unloving place. She vowed that one day, she'd provide a good life for Henry. She would not let him down.

There had been rumours for several days that men would come to St Margaret's Workhouse looking for apprentices and Keziah had bitten her nails to the quick, worrying that it would be the return of the master chimney sweeps who'd inspected the children the previous month and had eventually dragged away six boys – all of them sobbing. Everyone knew the terrible life young sweeps endured – constantly covered from head to toe in soot and sent up confined chimneys, often to their death through suffocation. Thankfully, Henry hadn't been selected as he was considered too weak and puny but one day he would grow and then what might happen? How would she be able to bear it?

However, these new rumours suggested the visitors wouldn't be grimy master sweeps, but gentlemen of quality, and their arrival would mean a change in fortune for many of the children. Not that Keziah believed the whispers. They were too good to be true and she knew beyond all doubt that no one was interested in her or Henry unless they stood to gain something.

Nevertheless, the mood of optimism fuelled by Mr Welch, the churchwarden, was hard to ignore. He'd spoken to the children after breakfast on the day the visitors were due at the workhouse and predictably, he'd warned them to be on their best behaviour when the gentlemen arrived at eight o'clock, but in hitherto unheard confidential tones, he'd added that the children were about to be offered a wonderful opportunity to learn how to become ladies and gentlemen. He'd continued by saying their visitors would not force anyone to go with them, so those wise children who could recognise a fine opportunity would need to show their willingness by signing or making their mark in the gentleman's book.

Shortly after, Mr Clegg entered the dining hall, followed by the taller of the two visitors who was dressed in dark green breeches and matching thigh-length cutaway coat over a beige waistcoat. The other man was older and more sombrely dressed in black, with a powdered, grey wig. The Master introduced them as Mr Rigby, owner of the Linderbourne Mill and his clerk, Mr Norris. The elder man had several ledgers tucked under his arm which he placed on the table, then sitting down, he opened them with an air of expectation.

In an unfamiliar accent, Mr Rigby addressed the hushed children, telling them he wanted to invite them to become his apprentices and to work in his cotton mill. In return, he would house, feed and ultimately train the boys to make stockings and the girls to make lace, so that when they reached the age of twenty-one and had served their apprenticeship, they would find well-paid employment. He would, however, only take the most conscientious and diligent boys and girls to work for him but in return, they would be given the opportunity to earn a good living. "Linderbourne," he added, "is north of Nottingham. It's a grand place and all my workers benefit from the fresh, healthy, clean air in the countryside. So, who would like to join us?"

Surely, Keziah reasoned, anything would be better than the workhouse? A heavy feeling drew at her insides, suppose she should be chosen but not Henry – or the other way around? How could she bear being separated from her brother? He was the only reason her life was worth living. Henry was small and wiry, but although she knew him to be strong, he didn't appear so. Sweat broke out on her brow and she allowed her shoulders to slump in an attempt to appear smaller and weaker as the gaze of the two gentlemen swept across them.

Keziah realised she'd been holding her breath and not listening when she became aware of his words, "If you would like to work for me, step forward now and see my clerk Mr Norris..."

So, Mr Welch had been correct and Mr Rigby wasn't going to select children – he was asking for volunteers. She glanced at the boys but without craning her neck she couldn't see Henry and she wondered whether he would step forward or not. She was sure he would be trying to gauge her reaction too. Mr Rigby invited the boys first and most of them went forward including Henry who risked a look over his shoulder. Their eyes met and Keziah gave him an imperceptible nod. She surreptitiously moved to the front of the group, hoping that if the girls were invited to volunteer too, she could make it to the table to speak to Mr Norris first. Now Henry had committed himself, she simply must be allowed to go with him. She dared not run nor push, for fear of being sent to the back of the line but with her head down, she managed to lose herself in the crowd of girls who pressed towards the table to add their names to the list. She was third in line to give her name to Mr Norris and to quickly sign her name where he indicated.

After their final breakfast in St Margaret's Workhouse, Mrs Clegg, on behalf of the parish, gave each child a parting gift of two new sets of clothes – one for workdays and one for Sundays, as well as a handkerchief, one shilling and a piece of gingerbread. Mr Clegg, who was in unusually good spirits, urged them to remember how much they owed the parish and to always do their duty to God and their betters. Those children who'd been sent to the workhouse by impoverished families were allowed five minutes to say goodbye to relatives who'd come to wave them off, while orphans like Keziah and Henry waited with teary eyes, wishing they, too, had someone to cling to – someone who cared.

At the ringing of Mr Clegg's bell, the eager children filed out of the dining hall while the beadles lined up with their long, strong staves at the ready. It was whispered they were forming a guard of honour but Keziah suspected that wasn't true. The men's faces betrayed determination, not celebration, as if their job was to ensure the boys and girls left – not to salute them – and if she was correct, it wouldn't have been surprising. The workhouse was overflowing, with new people arriving daily and the parish's struggling finances would benefit greatly from their departure. It would also explain Mr Clegg's good mood.

"Poor bairns!" Cook whispered to Martha as the children were lined up. "Like wee lambs to the slaughter," she added and Martha nudged her sharply with a shush.

But none of the children other than Keziah who'd been standing next to the nurse, heard, because of the excited hubbub. Cook's comments added to Keziah's gnawing anxiety and despite the other children assuming their new life would be better, she wondered if they were merely exchanging the hated workhouse for somewhere as bad or, heaven forbid, even worse. If only Eva were there to ask. Well, it was too late now – their signatures were in Mr Rigby's book. Not that she would have shared her fears with Henry who was caught up with the others in the joyful atmosphere and anyway, who was to say they weren't heading towards a better life? She was reasonably certain Mr Welch had only told them they'd be elevated to become ladies and gentlemen to persuade them to sign Mr Rigby's book and relieve the parish of the financial burden of keeping them. But surely one day, Fortune would favour them.

Messrs Osgood and Wilson, the two overlookers Mr Rigby had sent with the cart and driver glowered silently at the children they were to accompany on the journey to Linderbourne Mill. The would-be apprentices had spilt out of the workhouse gate, giggling and jostling, although their high spirits were quelled slightly under the menacing scrutiny of Mr Rigby's overlookers, the shorter of whom checked each child against his list as he counted them onto the back of the wagon. Once everyone was aboard, the beadles who'd followed the children strode back to the workhouse gate where they stood side by side as if forming a barrier to anyone who might at this late stage, change their mind and try to creep back into the workhouse. Next to the beadles, were three mothers. Each ragged woman was holding a baby on her hip. Various infants clutched at their aprons while the mothers sobbed into handkerchiefs and waved godspeed to the offspring who'd they'd previously sent to the workhouse. It would be many years before their son or daughter reached the age of twenty-one and therefore many years before any of them would see their child again – if ever.

At first, as the cart lurched and bounced through the early morning London streets, the new apprentices were so delighted to be setting off on such an exciting adventure, they sang and pushed handfuls of the straw that was the only cushioning on the floor of the cart, down each other's necks, shrieking with laughter. They called out joyfully to the early morning sellers; the milkmaids crying 'Mew!', others shouting 'Hot Pies!', 'Muffins! Muffins!' or 'Sweet China Oranges!', depending on their wares. As the cart trundled through streets redolent with the smells of cooking sausages, fresh coffee and baked bread that mingled with the stench from the River Fleet, Keziah finally gave herself up to the cheerful atmosphere and began to relax. No attempt had been made to arrange the children in the confined space of the cart, and now she was next to Henry feeling his arm pressed tightly against hers, and she joined in happily with the singing.

But several hours later, having left the streets and alleys of London far behind, several of the children complained the jerking, bumping motion of the cart was making them feel sick and by the time they stopped that evening, most of them were subdued and uncomfortable after hours of being shaken on the rutted, country roads.

They slept in the wagon that night, using what straw remained, and their bundles of new clothes as pillows and blankets but the cramped conditions and the novelty of sleeping under the stars prevented much sleep – despite their tiredness. By early morning, a damp, grey mist had enveloped them and exhaustion prompted several of the youngest to snivel and wish they'd never left London. Keziah was tired and aching, having spent an uncomfortable night sitting up, cradling Henry's head in her lap and shortly after they set off, the lurching, jolting motion of the wagon made her feel nauseous too.

"Is it much further?" Henry whispered. But Keziah had no idea.

# Chapter Two

On the fifth morning of their journey, they awoke stiff and cold, with hollow, growling stomachs. They'd been lucky to have found a kind farmer who'd allowed them to sleep in his barn overnight. Mr Wilson handed out the food that had been left over from the previous evening and they climbed aboard the cart once again in the pre-dawn light, shivering and bruised from the previous days' travel. Spirits rose slightly, however, when the driver told them that if all was well, they'd arrive in Linderbourne later that day.

Nevertheless, even that news wasn't sufficient to compensate for the sickening lurching motion of the wagon as it moved north of Nottingham. It rumbled along atrocious roads with ruts so deep, they were thrown about, colliding with the sides of the wagon and each other. Each child had his or her share of bruises, bumps and scrapes. Even the men were forced to hold on tightly to remain in their seats. Keziah wondered what would happen if a wheel came off or broke. They were flanked on either side by dense woodland and they'd passed very few vehicles or people since they'd left the barn. How long would they have to wait before a wheel could be repaired? Most likely, they'd have to finish the journey on foot. Keziah clung on as the wagon pitched forwards into a hole, then jolted up the other side. A walk, however long it took, might be preferable to this and she wondered at the wisdom of wishing a wheel would break. But against all odds, they remained intact.

Occasionally, the woods thinned out, to show fields of grazing animals that extended to the rolling hills in the distance. But mostly, their view of the surrounding countryside was concealed by the forest. Or perhaps there was nothing to conceal. Possibly, this part of England was completely covered by trees. One didn't have to walk far from the middle of London to see the surrounding countryside – didn't people drive herds and flocks from their farms to Smithfield Market to sell? But forests... Keziah had never seen anything so sinister with their tangled undergrowth and dark, threatening depths. Perhaps it was as well that the wagon wheels hadn't broken.

After several hours, the road began to climb and as the horses tired, the cart's progress slowed. Eventually, as they neared the top, the animals seemed to find the energy to crest the hill as if they knew the next part of the journey would be easier. Below them in a valley, the children spied a village with neat cottages lying along the banks of a river. Some way off on the right, on slightly higher ground, stood a grand mansion, overlooking the valley and village. As the oppressive clouds that had accompanied them from London thinned to reveal patches of blue sky, sunlight poured through, bathing the village in golden light and sparkling on the river.

"Linderbourne," the driver called over his shoulder.

At their approach, three dogs came out to greet them, barking and running back and forth. They loped alongside, tongues lolling until they reached the main road that ran through the village where they gave chase to some outraged chickens, sending them clucking and flapping into a garden. Several women holding young children in their arms or on hips stood at their doors, silently watching the cart go by.

At the far end of the neat rows of shops and cottages, was a coaching inn, a village green and the church. At this point, was a crossroads. To the left, lay a stone bridge that spanned the river and to the right, a road that seemed to head towards the mansion they'd spotted from the hilltop. Straight ahead, the road narrowed significantly as if it didn't lead anywhere important.

Judging by the wheel ruts, most vehicles that entered the village turned left to cross the river. Not surprising, as on the other side, was Linderbourne Mill. Keziah had seen more impressive buildings in London but this four-storey, red brick building with its dozens of mullioned windows on each floor and its bell tower was huge by comparison to the buildings in the village that shared its name. And that seemed to lend it an air of grandeur. Even from across the river, the hum and whir of machinery could be heard clearly as if the mill were a living, breathing being.

"All them machines in the mill, is driven by that waterwheel," the driver said proudly as if the mechanism belonged to him, "An' that mill is where you poor, wretched cubs will be a-slavin'—"

Mr Osgood elbowed him sharply and told him to keep his comments to himself at which the driver subsided into low grumbles and urged his horses straight ahead, along the narrow lane. Several minutes later, as he slowed the tired beasts, Keziah and Henry saw their new home – the Apprentice House.

"It looks like St Margaret's," Henry said, his lip curled in distaste as he took in the wide, two-storey building with the bell tower perched on the roof.

Keziah's chest tightened as she saw his disappointment and she tried to soothe his fears. "But look, my love, there's no wall and no gate to lock us in."

The cart turned off the road onto the drive that led to the imposing building and behind that, open fields swept up onto the hills.

"That's true," said Henry appearing to regain his enthusiasm. The sun was low in the sky and he squinted and shielded his eyes with one hand as he surveyed the forbidding building and scanned the surroundings for anything which might be used to lock them in, but there was nothing – no wall, no fence.

They appeared to be miles from anywhere, so what would be the point of attempting to escape? And where would they go, even if they did run away? They were prisoners, not because they were confined by walls but because of the vast distances between their new home and anywhere else. Despite the sunshine that was making a valiant effort to lend pink and peach tones to the grey, forbidding building in front of them, Keziah shivered and hoped Henry didn't notice.

Mr and Mrs Hagley, master and mistress of Apprentice House, were waiting for them at the main door, their faces impassive as the bedraggled group of dusty, tearstained children climbed down from the back of the cart, many exhausted and weak from motion sickness.

Mr Hagley led them into a dining hall filled with long tables flanked by benches and to Keziah's joy, she and Henry were allowed to sit where they liked after lining up at a hatch and being handed a bowl of thin milk porridge and a slice of rye bread.

The large room was laid out in a similar manner to the dining hall at St Margaret's, and it, too, had the familiar smell of stale food. However, overlying that, was an unpleasant odour Keziah couldn't identify. The strange, rancid stench did nothing to encourage the appetites of those children whose stomachs had been unsettled from the journey and were now churning again because of the smell. They stared balefully at their full bowls of unappetising porridge.

When voices and footsteps were heard from outside, Mrs Hagley opened the door and allowed in a large group of children; the girls dressed in stained pinafores and the boys in equally grimy shirts and trousers. All appeared to be covered in a layer of dust and here and there, on hair and clothes, were flecks of white fluff, like large snowflakes.

The newcomers eyed the recent arrivals from London with scorn and were keen to establish their superiority in the pecking order. If they had to share the Apprentice House, they wanted it to be acknowledged they were the experienced, and therefore more important members, of the apprentice community. However, several of them warmed to the new children considerably when they realised many of the bowls of porridge had been rejected and they eagerly took them and after adding the contents to their own food, they gobbled everything down quickly.

"You don't want to be wasting food," a pinched-faced boy said to one of the St Margaret's children, "We ain't given enough of it for that."

Keziah and Henry watched in dismay, both lost in their own thoughts; the food in the workhouse had been monotonous but at least there had always been sufficient.

Once the apprentices had finished eating, Mr Hagley addressed his charges and warned them against idleness, disobedience and insolence while tapping his outstretched palm with a horsewhip. This demonstration of the likely fate of anyone who didn't heed his words shocked the newcomers. In the workhouse, they'd been deprived of meals, forced to take on extra cleaning duties and shut in the dark but never had any of them been beaten. Now, wide eyes watched, trance-like, as the whip bounced up and down. Thwack, thwack, thwack.

When Mr Hagley had finished, he gathered the new boys together and led them upstairs to show them their beds while his wife took the girls to the other end of the building, to their dormitories. There were a dozen beds in the room to which Keziah had been assigned; each slept twenty-four girls.

Before the bell rang for bed, the apprentices were allowed to wander on the fields at the back of the Apprentice House and Keziah rushed to find Henry.

"I looked out the window and there are no walls or fences anywhere," he said in wonder, gazing across the fields to the gently sloping hills in the distance. "We could just walk and walk in that direction. But Mr Hagley said we're not allowed in the woods opposite the Apprentice House. They belong to Mr Rigby and he has man traps in there to keep out poachers."

The thought of being deep inside a wood filled Keziah with dread. The nearest she'd ever been to a forest was on the journey to Linderbourne and that had been close enough. Now, her heart thrummed when she imagined how dark and forbidding it would be.

They hadn't wandered far when the clanging of the bell in the tower rang out, calling them back to the house for bedtime. Keziah left Henry at the staircase to the boys' dormitories at one end of the building and joined the girls' queue at the other. Once in the room where she was to sleep, she discovered she was to share a bed with a pretty girl called Becky Ingham, who told her she'd been working at the mill for over a year.

"Well at least you ain't a big one," Becky remarked and Keziah quailed under the elder girl's critical stare.

"I reckon we'll do well enough," said Becky finally, with a satisfied nod.

She began to undress. "It's the smell of the oil what lubricates the machines," she said conversationally when she saw Keziah wrinkle her nose and frown. "Don't worry, you'll get used to it when you're covered in it too." She dropped her clothes on the floor next to their cot and climbed under the blanket.

"You'd best hasten," Becky said, "You won't never get enough sleep if you tarry like that." Within minutes, she was gently snoring.

Keziah curled up next to her new bedfellow but despite her weariness, sleep was slow to come and she lay awake for several hours after the candles had been snuffed. It wasn't the noise that kept her awake despite her exhaustion, on the contrary, it was the silence. Of course, there were snores and snufflings from the sleeping girls in the dormitory while outside, in the distance, an owl hooted. But there were no footsteps, no horses' hoofbeats, no jangling harnesses nor trundling of wheels on gravel, no raucous singing nor drunken shouts urging on a fight. The lack of those familiar sounds left her feeling strangely alone. Was this homesickness? She doubted it, for she had no longing at all to return to St Margaret's Workhouse. It must simply be fear of the unknown.

On the morrow, she and Henry would discover what sort of work they would be doing for the next few years and what manner of people they would be working for. It occurred to her that this was a new start and therefore the perfect time for her to change. Henry had shown maturity and had kept himself out of trouble. Now, she would try to tame her temper and thereby avoid attracting the wrong sort of attention. After all, it would be eleven years before she'd fulfil her obligations to Mr Rigby by which time she'd have been taught how to make lace and would be able to earn a fair wage. Then, when Henry was free, they would look after each other. But first, she had to learn to guard her tongue and to think before acting.

*You'd want me to change for the better, wouldn't you, Eva?*

Keziah's last thoughts as she drifted into sleep were of her sister, far away on the other side of the world. Or perhaps listening to her from heaven.

It only seemed like ten minutes later, when the iron door into the dormitory creaked and Mrs Hagley entered ringing a handbell. Keziah felt the mattress move as Becky scrambled out of bed. She prodded Keziah. "You'll get up if you know what's good for you," she said, her voice muffled as she pulled her shift over her head.

"You!" Mrs Hagley shouted from the door, "Get dressed immediately!"

It wasn't clear whom she was addressing as all the workhouse girls had been slow to react. Keziah squeezed her eyes together tightly, trying to banish sleep and pulled on her clothes, as she followed Becky from the dormitory, down to the pump to wash.

Had the closely-cropped heads of the workhouse children not marked them out from the seasoned apprentices, it would still have been obvious from their sleepy faces and yawns. The day had never begun so early in St Margaret's and many of the children had not recovered from the arduous journey. Ten minutes was allowed for a simple breakfast, then the experienced apprentices set off along the road towards the mill followed by the newcomers.

"We will be happy, won't we, Kezzie?" Henry said, taking a skip and jump to keep up with her.

"We'll make the best of it, I'm sure." She filled her voice with a confidence she didn't feel.

"I hope we don't have to work with Mr Osgood. I don't like him. He's got cold eyes."

"Well, it could be worse. At least he hasn't forced us to listen to him read the Bible."

Henry giggled.

Keziah, too, had misgivings about the dark, hook-nosed man with the steely eyes. Henry was right, there was something menacing about him.

How different this was from London. The air smelt so fresh, it seemed to make Keziah's nostrils tingle after the grimy, smoky atmosphere she was used to. Birds sang from deep inside the woods where the sound of gushing water was occasionally disturbed by a splash as an animal dived into the river.

As they approached the crossroad, the hum of the machinery inside the mill began to drown the sounds of the countryside. The rhythmic beat grew in intensity as they walked over the bridge towards the enormous building. Once they'd been ushered inside, the smell Becky had said was machine oil, increased to sickening proportions. Cotton particles hung in the air, some so fine they were like dust, while others were as large as snowflakes that fluttered down to the wooden floor, irritating eyes, throats and nostrils.

The established apprentices rushed away; some scampering up the stairs, others entering the room on the ground floor, leaving the new children with Mr Rigby and Mr Osgood, the surly overlooker.

Mr Rigby welcomed the children. "At Linderbourne Mill, I pride myself on care for my workers. As well as board, you will receive several hours schooling per week that will take place in the evening after work. You will start work promptly at five-thirty in the morning and finish at eight in the evening with one hour allowed for dinner. If, for any reason, the waterwheel stops, every minute will be made up as soon as the machinery is running again. And woe betide anyone who arrives late. The door to each room will be locked by its overlooker at five-thirty and anyone not inside by that time will have to make up the hours out of their own time."

Own time? With work, school and church on Sundays, there would be precious little of that.

Keziah stood next to Henry linking her little finger with his. If they remained close, then perhaps they'd be sent to the same place to work and she'd be able to look after him. Mr Rigby raised his arm and in a downward, sweeping motion like an axe falling, he divided the children into two. Keziah held her breath as she watched the hand arc through the air, then sagged with relief. She and Henry were both included in the same group. They each squeezed the other's little finger in celebration.

The master took the first group into the room on the ground floor and Mr Osgood led the group containing the two Bonner children to the second floor. The roar of the machinery reverberated through the building, echoing in the stairwell and as they climbed higher the cotton fibres in the air increased, filling their nostrils and making Henry cough.

"Kezzie?" he croaked and when she saw his eyes bright with tears, she touched the tip of her nose. Not – this time – to tell him she was well but to persuade him all would be fine. The air was thick with cotton fibres on the stairs and she hoped the many windows she'd noticed on each floor would allow air to circulate and to clear the rooms.

Once on the second floor, Mr Osgood removed the large bunch of keys from his belt and opened the door. Henry and Keziah were at the front of the band of children and they recoiled. If anything, the air was thicker with cotton fluff inside the long room than it had been on the stairs and they peered disbelievingly at the men, women and children who were moving with purpose in what appeared to be a blizzard from which came the roar of machinery and the overpowering stench of lubricating oil.

It seemed that Mr Osgood was looking for an opportunity to demonstrate his authority, so when Henry gasped and took a step backwards, Mr Osgood gave him a blow to the side of the head which knocked him into Keziah.

"Get used to it!" he growled and pushed his face close to Henry's.

"Do you have a problem?"

Henry flinched and gave a slight shake of his head. His eyes were wide with fear. "No, sir," he whispered.

Nobody dared speak but all eyes were on Mr Osgood, who slowly drew back, his eyes boring into Henry. With a jerk of his head, he indicated the new apprentices should enter.

It was unlike anything Keziah had experienced before. The room was long and filled with strange machines that workers pushed back and forth. As they did so, threads were pulled out from the thick, soft untwisted ropes of cotton fibre and then spooled onto countless bobbins. Suspended below the ceiling, were continually rotating shafts that ran the length of the entire room. At intervals along these, leather belts extended down to the machines to drive them. Here and there, apprentices took full bobbins from the spinning frames and replaced them with empty ones, while others crawled beneath the constantly moving machines parts to clean up waste cotton. But everywhere, was noise and bustle, all dusted with the fibres that were relentlessly discharged into the air.

Henry caught Keziah's eye and raised his eyebrows. She was too shocked to respond by either touching her nose or her ear. There were no words – nor signs – to express her horror.

By the end of the day, Keziah's eyes were red-rimmed and sore. Her throat was hoarse with the clogging cotton particles and she ached from creeping under the moving frames to clean up. Henry seemed as dejected as his sister as the bell rang at eight and they wearily descended the stairs to return to the Apprentice House, leaving behind the still whirring and clacking machines. Keziah was so exhausted, she couldn't bring herself to voice her thoughts and Henry was silent too. No words were needed. Henry must be aware, as was she, they had exchanged the workhouse for something much worse.

# CHAPTER THREE

1794:

The early spring rains had swollen the Linderbourne River, almost submerging the stepping stones over which Keziah crossed from the mill to the opposite bank on her way to the Apprentice House. The headrace that had been built to ensure a constant supply of water to turn the gigantic waterwheel, and therefore keep the mill's machinery working, had almost overflowed its banks. However, that was preferable to the previous two summers when the water had been so low at times, the wheel had stopped. The first time it had happened Keziah and Henry discovered it meant working late into the night and rising much earlier in the morning until all the work had been done.

But now the water was more than sufficient to drive the wheel and since Keziah shouldn't have been crossing the river in the middle of Mr Rigby's woods, she could hardly complain about her wet boots. Damp feet, however, were the least of her worries and she knew she'd be in serious trouble should she be caught. Not that the master's gamekeepers spent much time there because the area of trees was relatively small compared to the rest of the Linderbourne Hall estate. Besides, Keziah was certain that few animals would choose to live so close to the constant whirring, clacking and humming of the mill. So, who would bother attempting to poach? There were better pickings in the large forest on the other side of the mansion.

Keziah had been shown the shortest route between the mill and the Apprentice House by her bedfellow, Becky, although she'd been reluctant at first to enter the woods – particularly on her own. But often, it was necessary to snatch time from somewhere and increasingly, she'd become used to the subdued green light and the peace of the forest as she hastily took a shortcut. Not that she lingered. There was never time.

Becky had shown her several paths through the trees, having explored them extensively with her young man, Peter. Keziah knew exactly what Becky and Peter were up to when they slipped away to meet in the woods and she made sure an embarrassed Henry understood too, despite his protests that he didn't need to hear such things. But how could she protect him if he was totally ignorant of life? Knowledge was armour.

Years before, their sister, Eva, had shielded Keziah from the details that daughters of families in the middling class didn't need to know until their wedding day. She'd obviously believed she'd acted in her younger sister's interest but Keziah often wondered if things would have been different had she been more worldly-wise. It was unlikely Eva would have been able to keep them out of the workhouse but at least they'd have been together.

It had started on the night the three children were lost and alone in London. Keziah had believed that Mrs Jenner, the elegant woman who'd befriended them, had offered them hospitality in her mansion, out of goodness and generosity. How could Keziah possibly have known the woman ran a high-class bawdy house and had instead, seen an opportunity to sell Eva's virginity to one of her customers? Eva had not suspected the truth either until she was faced with the man who'd bought her.

The conversation between the two sisters after Eva had returned to their room; her hair dishevelled and her face white with shock, would be forever etched in Keziah's memory.

"I can't do it, I simply can't!" Eva had said.

"Can't?" Keziah had spat at her, "I can't believe you're being so selfish! This is your chance to repay Mrs Jenner for her hospitality. You're always telling me off for thinking of myself and now you're doing just that! What can possibly be that bad?"

It had been much later that Keziah had discovered what could possibly be that bad, and then, she'd been bitterly ashamed of her foolish words.

But that had not been all the harm Keziah had caused. Eva had told her if they threw themselves on the mercy of the parish, they'd be sent to the workhouse and separated from Henry, but as usual, Keziah had assumed she knew better. After all, she'd reasoned, hadn't Papa always paid his parish dues promptly? Hadn't he given alms to the poor? Indeed, he had. Then the parish authorities would remember his willingness to assist the needy and they would make special provision for his children. How ludicrous that line of thinking now seemed. And because Keziah had defied her sister, the family had been broken apart. Eva had gone and she and Henry were as good as slaves, working exhausting hours with no prospect of release for years.

And that was why she was taking a shortcut through the woods with only fifteen minutes to wash, change out of her work clothes and get to the schoolhouse. She had a plan for the future – hers and Henry's – but it would need plenty of hard work and dedication, as well as punctuality.

As she crossed the leafy forest floor, her boots squelched from their drenching in the river and she glanced nervously about, wary of being caught but possibly more afraid of arriving at the schoolhouse late. Miss

Maynard, the schoolmistress would not tolerate tardiness nor untidiness and Keziah was desperate to make a good impression – especially that evening when Mrs Rigby would be there observing the lesson.

She'd been held up because her overlooker, Mr Osgood, had punished her and although he was aware she had permission to leave the mill thirty minutes early, he'd kept her late. She suspected the reason he often singled her out for punishment was that shortly after she'd arrived he'd noticed that she, of all the girls, had a spark of defiance and he delighted in demonstrating he was in control. But she'd become more determined each time he goaded her, to conquer her temper and she'd now learnt to compose her expression, glance down submissively and remain silent. During the last four years, she'd saved herself countless beatings and while she'd gained control over her impulsiveness, by a twist of fate, Henry, who'd started in the mill as well-behaved as he'd been in the workhouse, was now showing the family streak of defiance.

He'd been befriended by one of the older apprentices, Jack Lawley. It had started with a few forays into the woods when the boys had returned with scratched arms and their mouths stained with blackberry juice. During the cold, snowy winter, there hadn't been much opportunity for them to wander far without their footprints giving them away. But when the weather improved, Jack had acquired some cotton fabric and using a branch, he'd fashioned a net, of sorts, and the two boys had gone fishing in the river which ran through Mr Rigby's woods. Somehow, they'd caught a fish and had cooked it over a fire, returning in the morning just in time to start work. So far, the boys had been too clever to be caught. But it was just a matter of time and then their punishment would be severe. If they behaved too badly, Mr Rigby might even send Henry away and then her heart would break.

The thought made the breath catch in her throat and drove her on even faster until she was running, heedless of rabbit holes and tangled roots. Her plan would be a success and she would keep Henry safe. She was setting everything up so painstakingly and patiently, surely Fortune would respect her efforts and not snatch triumph away at the last moment?

Keziah had been singled out by the schoolmistress, because of her aptitude for reading, writing and arithmetic. She'd been selected by Miss Maynard to be her monitress to help during each evening's lesson and despite Keziah's exhaustion at the end of each day working in the mill, she'd desperately tried to impress the schoolmistress. Miss Maynard had let slip the fact that she was looking for advancement and desired a post as a governess in a great house and Keziah hoped that one day, she would become the schoolmistress in her place.

Currently, Mr Rigby's son was away at boarding school but his three daughters were taught in Linderbourne Hall by Miss Price, an elderly governess who suffered with fainting fits. Miss Maynard was taking great pains to impress Mrs Rigby and gain favour in the hope that one day she would be engaged to teach her daughters.

It was unlikely Mrs Rigby, who had taken a special interest in the mill's school, would consider Keziah as a schoolmistress because of her youth. But recently, Miss Maynard had hinted that if she were to recommend Keziah, it might, indeed, be a possibility.

In the meantime, Keziah was afforded special privileges which allowed her to carry out her duties as school monitress – one of which was to be allowed out of work early so she could be ready for school.

A noise from her right sent waves of panic rushing through her and she crouched, pressing herself into the depths of a bush, oblivious to the prickles and spikes.

A twig cracked.

Leaves rustled.

A horse whinnied and stamped a hoof.

But no one approached.

Straining to hear above the throbbing of her pulse, she realised whoever she'd heard was not coming nearer. In fact, the sounds suggested the person was lying on the ground, hidden behind a large tree trunk about ten paces away. Low moans suggested someone was in pain, possibly having been thrown from the horse.

*What should I do?*

Only a member of the Rigby family would be riding through Linderbourne Hall land, so if she revealed herself, there would be serious repercussions. On the other hand, if she crept away...

She took a deep breath and quietly disentangled herself from the clutching, clawing bush. If she inched across the mossy bank, she might be able to assess how badly hurt the rider was without showing herself and with luck, he would even now, be mounting the horse ready to ride away.

Keziah was so intent on avoiding twigs and stepping silently, she'd reached the large tree trunk when she realised there was not one but two people on the ground – one on top of the other.

Her hand flew to her mouth to stifle a gasp of surprise, and anger coursed through her as she assumed it was Becky and Peter who'd given her such a fright. But this girl's hair was blonde and the man was much slimmer than Peter. And neither of them owned a horse. Before Keziah could turn away, the girl's eyes opened and for a second, they stared at each other, then, with cheeks aflame, Keziah fled, relieved she'd merely stumbled over two lovers meeting secretly in the woods but irritated they'd made her even later.

The foolish girl's face wasn't familiar but perhaps she didn't work in the mill. Mr Rigby had built cottages and facilities for his workers in the village but not everyone in Linderbourne was employed in the mill. The girl was obviously one of those.

Keziah arrived back at the Apprentice House, her heels chafed by the wet leather and her throat parched after a day breathing in cotton fibres and her dash through the woods. After washing and carefully combing the cotton fluff from her hair she hurriedly pulled on her Sunday clothes. She'd never arrived to assist Miss Maynard in her soiled work clothes because she'd wanted to demonstrate how seriously she took the post.

As she hurried along the road from the Apprentice House, she prayed the church clock wouldn't chime the quarter-hour before she arrived at the schoolhouse because if she could make it by 7:45, then Miss Maynard wouldn't be angry.

The chimes began as she opened the door but unusually, the large room was empty. Keziah went back to the schoolyard gate to look along the main road through the village. There was no sign of the schoolmistress, so she prepared for the evening's lessons, ready for Miss Maynard when she arrived. Having opened the windows, arranged the lamps and placed the slates on the tables, Keziah was neatening Miss Maynard's desk and wondering what to do next when she heard a noise outside the door. She hurried to open it and found the schoolmistress with her hair in disarray, her bonnet hanging around her neck by its ribbons, trying to brush the dust and dead leaves off her skirt with the back of her hands.

Keziah gasped when she noticed the older woman's palms were both bleeding. "Miss Maynard! What happened?"

"No need to fuss, my dear, I simply tripped." She winced as she straightened up and Keziah hesitantly offered her arm, not knowing if the prim schoolteacher would find such forwardness inappropriate. But it appeared that such behaviour was indeed acceptable and Miss Maynard took her arm and hobbled to her chair. Keziah ran to the pump in the yard and filled a jug with water for Miss Maynard to wash her hands.

Although nothing was broken and the only damage appeared to be to the palms of her hands and her dignity, Miss Maynard was obviously shaken and her usual reserve crumbled.

Taking Keziah into her confidence, she said, "It's my knees and ankles, you see. They swell so, in the damp weather. As I crossed the road, I stepped over a rut and I was caught a little off balance. I went down so heavily on my hands and knees. I'm sorry, Keziah, but I'm afraid I'm too indisposed to take the class tonight and my knee has swollen to twice its normal size, so you'll have to take the lessons."

"Take the lessons?" Keziah was both delighted and appalled.

This was a great opportunity as Mrs Rigby would be there to observe how well the school that she considered her own project was being run.

Keziah tried to swallow but her mouth was completely dry. If only she'd had time to prepare. But what could she have done even if she'd known in advance? She'd simply have worried. No, after a sip of water, she'd be fine. She must be fine.

There was no choice. The children had already started to line up at the door having come straight from the mill and there were loud exclamations as the clip-clop of horses' hooves and crunch of carriage wheels heralded the arrival of Mrs Rigby from Linderbourne Hall.

"You will be marvellous," Miss Maynard said, "and I will advise, should you need it."

Under the critical gaze of Miss Maynard and Mrs Rigby, her thoughts which she'd managed to get into order, now scattered like cotton dust in the wind. She took another sip of water.

Even worse, as the children had entered, she'd been trying so hard to take everything in, she'd taken in nothing, and as a result, Henry was sitting next to Jack Lawley. She knew she should separate them but now all the desks were taken and she didn't want to disrupt the lesson and draw attention to her brother. He'd become quite thoughtless of late and had been taking more notice of Jack than of her. Surely Henry would appreciate her difficult position and cooperate?

"Good evening, children. Please greet your benefactress," Miss Maynard said.

"Good evening, ma'am," the children chorused and Keziah saw Jack nudge Henry and laugh. She glared at him but he didn't look her way.

Miss Maynard nodded at Keziah. "You may begin the lesson, Miss Bonner."

Keziah took a deep breath. "Susan Williams, please come forward and recite the piece you were set last lesson."

Miss Maynard looked relieved, Mrs Rigby looked interested and Susan Williams looked panic-stricken.

The lesson progressed with each child coming forward to recite the passage from the Bible which they had learnt and Keziah was relieved that Henry recited without hesitation.

She wrote a sum on the board and one of each pair wrote on the slate they shared, then they worked together. Keziah noticed that Henry was barely stifling his laughter and she casually strolled towards the back of the schoolhouse to prevent Henry from causing trouble, although, she acknowledged he most certainly deserved to be punished. She was appalled he could be so thoughtless as to jeopardise her chance to impress Mrs Rigby and Miss Maynard.

True, she hadn't discussed her dream of becoming a schoolmistress with him because it had been too fragile an idea to put into words. But she deserved more thought than he was obviously giving her at the moment. By the time she arrived at Henry's desk Jack had rubbed out whatever it was Henry had found amusing and their heads were together as they pored over the sum. Henry looked up and Keziah pulled her earlobe, using their sign language to convey to him something was wrong. Henry's expression collapsed. She knew he was contrite but it was hard for him to behave while sitting next to Jack who had little interest in numbers and letters. Nevertheless, he resisted Jack's nudges until the other boy gave up trying to distract him.

Eventually, the lesson ended and, ignoring Keziah, Mrs Rigby spoke to Miss Maynard, "I notice the children need to share slates. It is quite unsatisfactory, and I shall remedy the situation immediately. I shall ask my husband to provide more."

Miss Maynard smiled broadly and cast a satisfied glance at Keziah, who heaved a huge sigh of relief as it appeared that despite Henry and Jack testing her patience, she'd proved adequate to the task.

Mrs Rigby insisted she convey Miss Maynard to her cottage in the village and suggested she did not return to work until she felt able.

"Miss... er... Barker, is it? Ah, yes, Bonner. Well, Miss Bonner can take over while you are indisposed, Miss Maynard. She seems to be adequate, despite her youth."

As soon as Mrs Rigby had swept out followed by Miss Maynard leaning on the arm of a footman, the children ran out of the school. Everyone was keen to get back to the Apprentice House for supper, leaving Keziah on her own to tidy. Usually, Henry waited for her but he'd obviously gone with Jack. She hoped they'd go directly home but she suspected they'd take the opportunity to go into the woods and... well, who knew what mischief they'd get up to? She worried about them catching fish and lighting fires – surely the height of foolishness. One day, the smoke would be smelt or seen and they'd be discovered.

Recently, Becky had told her they'd been seen loitering near the tavern and it was thought several bottles of gin had been stolen. Keziah felt as though the breath had been squeezed out of her. As soon as she saw Henry, she'd take him to one side forbid him to go out with Jack again. He was putting himself in dreadful danger. But she was rarely alone with him these days and she dared not risk anyone else hearing the conversation she must have with him. The fewer people who knew Henry had been trespassing – and perhaps thieving, the better.

She pressed each temple with a forefinger and closed her eyes. Deep inside, she knew his behaviour was her fault. Once again, she'd let her family down. She'd concentrated so hard on her ambitions, she'd allowed Henry to run wild. It must stop. She tidied away the slates and extinguished the lamps before leaving the school for the night.

Once she'd closed the door, she peered through the darkness for Henry. She hoped he might have come back for her so they could walk home together. Although he'd never admitted it, she knew the time he'd been locked in a cupboard in the workhouse still horrified him but usually, he'd brave his fears to wait for her. But not that night. It would be just like Jack to demand he made up for refusing to misbehave in school and her stomach sank when she imagined them in the woods. She knew Henry didn't like going out with Jack at night but just lately, something was driving him on. Perhaps it was because he wanted to hit back at those in authority.

It wasn't surprising. Mr Osgood, the overlooker, in the room where Henry was a cotton doffer, fixing cotton threads that had broken on the looms, was particularly cruel to Henry having taken a dislike to the young lad. It appeared that Henry's resentment was showing itself in defiance against anyone in charge.

"Foolish boy!" she muttered as she walked along the road back to the Apprentice House and then at a rustling in the undergrowth, she took fright and broke into a run, her boots still soaking wet and rubbing her heels.

One day she'd be able to afford another pair of boots and what's more, she'd have enough to keep herself and Henry safe.

# CHAPTER FOUR

Matthew Gregory was an exceptionally tolerant man. But really! Such behaviour from a manservant was entirely unacceptable.

And why was Jefferson's voice so shrill, it seemed to be slicing through his brain.

"Stop it," he mumbled, grabbing the sheet and pulling it back up to his chin.

A deluge of cold water on his face made him cry out, spluttering with indignation. He wiped his eyes with the sleeve of his nightgown. This was insufferable!

"At long last!" It was his sister, Lucy, standing next to his bed her arms crossed, the water jug that she'd just emptied over his head dangling from one hand and her eyes glinting angrily. "Get up!" she said in a disgusted tone. "You are a disgrace to the family!" And then she burst out laughing.

Matthew couldn't help but smile at her impersonation of their father.

"Go away, Luce! It's too early. I'm tired." His mouth was dry and tasted of stale brandy.

"Please, get up, Matt. I need your help."

His brain, although swirling with alcohol-muddled thoughts, detected the anxiety in her voice. Reluctantly, he sat up and winced as she pulled open the curtains, allowing bright, morning sunlight to flood in. "Lucy! Have you taken leave of your senses? It's only eleven o'clock! I told Jefferson not to wake me for another hour!" he said as he caught sight of the clock.

Lucy sat down on the silk cover of his bed and pulling a letter from her pocket, she unfolded it.

"Is it news of Father?" he asked, his eyes wide in alarm. She had his full attention now.

Sir Hugh Gregory, their father, had been as well as could be expected when Matthew had left London several days before, but his health was poor, and news from London was unlikely to be good. It certainly wouldn't have been a letter from Father, as he never wrote to Matthew or Lucy when they stayed in Linderbourne Hall with Uncle Obadiah – or indeed when they stayed anywhere. After their mother had died giving birth to Lucy, their father had become more remote than ever. Then, came Father's 'accident' always spoken of in hushed tones by Aunt Hannah, his sister, and after that, his life had slowed down considerably. While Father was alive and coping, Matthew could relax.

Sir Hugh's attention had been lavished on Matthew's elder brother, Robert, who would one day have succeeded to his father's baronetcy. Robert had been everything a father could want in a son – intelligent and strong – nothing like the dreamy, distracted second son, Matthew, who soon learnt that no matter what he did, he'd always be considered second best. Matthew had adored Robert who'd achieved everything he attempted, with little or no effort and it wasn't Robert's fault Father only noticed his elder son's successes. Matthew discovered the best way to avoid being unfavourably compared to his brother was to stop trying. To feign a lack of interest. To excel at apathy. It had infuriated his father which Matthew had found most satisfying until the day Father had insisted he choose a career in either the church or the army. Matthew had refused both and before his father could disown him, Uncle Obadiah Rigby had stepped in and financed further education at Oxford where, between the gaming tables and riotous parties, Matthew had found sufficient time to read Law.

Tragically, almost a year ago, Robert had died in a hunting accident and Sir Hugh had not yet come to terms with the loss – nor forgiven Matthew for not being Robert.

Matthew always dreaded news from London. One day, a letter would arrive informing Matthew the life he'd planned must be shelved in favour of his father's baronetcy which would make him Sir Matthew Gregory and demand he ran the family estates.

The life he had planned? That was a slight exaggeration as Matthew very rarely made arrangements in advance for anything other than the next ball he might attend or when he might go to his club.

What was the point? The closest he'd come to forming a life plan was to prevaricate for as long as possible. While his father was alive that was an option but on his death...

"No, it's not from London," Lucy said, shaking her head sadly and turning the letter over and over.

"Well, who's it from, then?" Matthew asked irritably. His tongue rasped against the roof of his mouth and his head felt as though it were full of the cotton that Uncle Obadiah's mill spun into thread.

"That's the problem, I don't know. Oh, Matthew, this is a disaster!"

With a resigned sigh, he held out his hand for the letter. The sooner he calmed her worries, the sooner she'd leave him in peace. Lucy hesitated then gave it to him.

He read in silence, his dark eyebrows drawing together and his eyes narrowing. "What nonsense!" Whoever had dared to write this to his sister would be in trouble when their uncle found out.

Lucy hung her head and ignored the letter he passed back to her.

Doubt squeezed his chest. "Luce? Is there any truth in this at all?"

Lucy jumped at his sharp tone. As she twisted the ring around her finger, Matthew knew it was, indeed, true and his younger sister was in trouble. His muddled thoughts sharpened with startling clarity. She needed his help and as the two neglected children of Sir Matthew Gregory, they were bound to each other. He'd do his best to make this go away. "Who delivered the letter?"

She shook her head, tears now perched on her lower eyelids. "I don't know," she whispered, "One of the maids found it outside the front door weighted down with a stone and she gave it to me. Anyone could have left it there."

"Your lover?"

"No!" said Lucy quickly, "Tom wouldn't do that to me."

"It says he's a carpenter at the mill. For heaven's sake, Luce!"

"You're a fine one to talk. What about that blonde—"

"I'm a man! You know the rules are different. They shouldn't be but they are. And anyway," he waved the sheet of paper at her, "I'm not being blackmailed. If you're sure it's not your carpenter, who else knows?"

"Nobody."

"Somebody must!"

"Well, there was a girl in the woods..."

"The woods? You were with the carpenter in the woods? Have you taken leave of your senses? What were you thinking?" Matthew pushed his fingers through his tousled, dark hair. It was still wet from his earlier dousing. "You know Aunt Hannah has been trying to arrange a good match for you. If this gets out you'll be ruined!"

"Yes, I am well aware of that!" snapped Lucy. "But everything here's so dull! You've only been in Linderbourne a few hours. I've been here a month and there's nothing to do! No hunt – well there is, but since Uncle and Aunt aren't fully accepted into society they're never invited and therefore neither am I. No balls – well, none that anyone thinks to ask me to. No theatres at all. There's nothing! Despite me being the daughter of Sir Hugh Gregory, in this godforsaken part of the country, I'm just the niece of Mr Rigby, the *mill* owner!"

"Lucy," Matthew said gently, placing his hand on hers, "I know you're used to being accepted in London society but it's different here. We both owe Uncle a lot. If it wasn't for him, we'd both be ruined. Remember, it's his mill that pays off the debts that Father, you and I run up."

There was a hard knot in his stomach as he remembered how much he owed after his last stay in London, and anticipating the conversation he'd shortly be having with his uncle who would surely reach new heights of fury.

However, Matthew's gambling debts would be as nothing compared to the discovery of his niece's liaison in the woods with a carpenter from his own mill. Uncle Obadiah prided himself on his strict morals and although he'd so far financially supported his wife's family, there must surely come a point when he decided his obligation had been paid in full. Then the house in London and Sir Hugh's country estates would have to be sold and he and Lucy would be... well his imagination couldn't serve him an adequate picture of what the future might hold.

He knew there was poverty around him; in London, he occasionally glimpsed that world as he glanced out of the carriage window. Travelling to or from his club or the theatre, he'd noticed the streets were filled with ragged paupers begging, men heaving enormous sacks of coal on their backs, people driving cattle to market or hauling barrows piled high with rags, not to mention the sellers of fish, fruit, flowers, cakes and pies; all with baskets of their wares balanced on their heads but Matthew soon forgot them when he arrived at his destination. The thought that he and his family would join the ranks of those unfortunates on the streets, or in a debtors' prison, was as unbelievable as the notion they might all sprout wings and fly away.

Everything needed to be handled with the utmost care.

*Think!* He squeezed his eyes shut tightly and tried to form a plan. "The girl," he said, "who is she?"

"I don't know."

"Are you certain she saw you?"

"Oh yes, I'm certain."

"You'd recognise her?"

"Yes, I believe so."

"Then we must find her. Could she be one of the maids?"

"I don't know. All Aunt's maids look the same to me, although..."

"Yes?"

"I think she was wearing one of those ghastly pinafores the mill girls wear. And it was fairly near the mill."

"Then, while I get ready, find some excuse to check all the women in the Hall and if you don't find her, we'll have breakfast and go down to the mill and look for her. Will the mill workers have started work yet, do you think?" He tugged the embroidered cord, ringing the bell to summon Jefferson.

"I've no idea. Whenever I've passed the mill, there always seem to be people there."

"She must live somewhere in this valley, so we'll find her."

"But what then? If I don't pay her, she'll tell everyone and I'll be ruined."

"Not necessarily," said Matthew, "after all, nobody is allowed in the woods so she was trespassing. So long as your carpenter keeps quiet, it's your word against hers. Who will Uncle believe?"

"But if she whispers in the wrong ear... Perhaps I should just pay her and hope that it's the end to the matter."

"Lucy! Blackmailers very rarely stop after the first payment. Do you have fifty guineas?"

Lucy shook her head. "I was hoping you had enough to lend me some money, Matthew."

"I'm sorry, Luce, I lost several times that sum, last weekend. Now, I have nothing other than what I can persuade Uncle to advance me. But recently, he's been making sure I have very little as he knows how good I am at spending it. I can only hope he'll cover the debts I've just run up." The knot in his stomach twisted at the thought of begging from his uncle. Again.

"Is that why you came to Linderbourne? I thought it strange you hadn't chosen to stay in London." She frowned at him. "Honestly, Matthew, if only you didn't spend so much time at the gaming tables and lavishing gifts on women! You wouldn't have to beg Uncle for money."

"And if only you hadn't gone in the woods with a carpenter!"

The brother and sister glared at each other.

Lucy backed down first, "I'm sorry Matt, I didn't mean to criticise. It's just that I feel so wretched."

"I'm sorry too, Luce. And I will help you manage this situation. Hush now, Jefferson will be here shortly. We will find her don't worry."

"And then what shall we do?"

"Leave that to me." Matthew's voice was confident but in truth, he had very little idea.

# Chapter Five

Keziah jumped and nearly knocked the lamp over as the latch on the schoolhouse door rattled.

Had one of the apprentices come back for something they'd forgotten? That was unlikely, as Keziah had already made sure everything was clean and ready for the following day. Only one lamp was lit and she was about to carry it to the door, then extinguish the flame and leave the schoolhouse for the night, so she hoped it wouldn't mean searching for something small in the dark.

But when the door flew open crashing into the wall, Keziah nearly dropped the lamp in fright.

A well-dressed man wearing riding clothes – a dark frock coat and lighter breeches – stood there with his hat tucked beneath his arm. He tapped the side of his boot with a riding crop as he took in the schoolroom.

She wondered if this could be Mr Rigby's son. But wasn't he still at school? This was definitely a man. His face was in shadow but she could see enough of his firm chin with its slight show of stubble to know he wasn't a boy. This was a man in his twenties, she guessed. A man with an air of entitlement.

Having glanced from left to right he strode towards her. She checked how far she was from the poker at the fireplace and wondered if she ought to pick it up. As he drew closer to the lamp she was holding up, she could see his expression was menacing

"Miss Bonner?" His voice was imperious and caught her off-guard. How did he know her name?

"Yes, sir," she said, squaring her shoulders and trying to hold her voice steady.

He nodded curtly. "Pray allow me to introduce myself. I am Matthew Gregory, nephew of your employer, Mr Rigby. I have come to offer you a word of advice. First, you must understand my uncle has many influential friends, none of whom would offer you employment, should you be dismissed—"

Dismissed? A thousand thoughts swirled in Keziah's mind. Why should she be dismissed?

The man continued, "Nobody who threatens any member of the Rigby family will emerge unscathed. I must confess, I had expected someone with more presence... but appearances can sometimes be deceptive. Nevertheless, I have come to inform you, your demands will not be met and should you be foolish enough to carry out your threat, you will lose your reputation your livelihood and your home – I will personally see to that…"

He paused, his eyes boring into her in a way that suggested she should understand and take heed. Her silence and puzzled expression appeared to disarm him. "Have I not made my position clear, Miss Bonner?"

Coming at the end of a day where Mr Osgood had kept her working during dinner time so she hadn't eaten since that morning, she now felt irritable and reckless. And worse, despite her pleas to Henry to behave well in school, especially while she was in charge, Jack had once again that evening taken advantage of the absence of Miss Maynard and had persuaded Henry to torment the girl sitting in front of them. Jack seemed to have accurately guessed that Keziah would be reluctant to reprimand or indeed punish Henry and that would allow him to act with impunity.

She might have been able to put her resentment against Henry and her hunger-pangs in perspective but she was also exhausted. The previous night, Becky had returned to their bed during the early hours, waking Keziah. And now this arrogant, young man had hurled open the school door and was haranguing her. True, he knew her name but he'd obviously mistaken her for someone else. It was too much. Despite promising herself she'd keep her temper under control, his angry accusations and threats were like sparks falling on tinder.

Before she'd had a chance to think, she'd taken a deep breath and with a set jaw and nostrils flared, words flew out of her mouth, "Sir! I believe you are mistaken! I have threatened no one, neither do I intend to. I do, however, intend to blow out this lamp and then I am going home. What you do after that, is your concern!"

She put the lamp down on the desk carefully, aware her hands were shaking with fury. Or was it fear? A little of both, perhaps.

His eyebrows drew together but not, as she might have assumed, in anger. His lips twitched slightly and he seemed mildly amused; almost puzzled.

Her words hadn't been rude but she knew no one who worked in the mill should speak to a member of the Rigby family in such a disagreeable manner.

Well, it was too late for regrets now. It took so long to build up people's trust but how quickly it could be lost. She swallowed and fought back the tears which she knew would come as soon as he left to find his uncle and report her rudeness. But other than tapping his boot with his crop thoughtfully, he didn't move.

"Miss Bonner," he said in polite but cold tones, "that was very prettily said, I'm sure. In fact, you almost convinced me... but I happen to know for certain that you are the culprit."

Her fingernails dug into her palms as her anger reignited. She stepped towards him, "Culprit? Culprit of *what*? I have done nothing! Except work and work and *work*!" The last word was almost strangled in her throat as she fought to keep the tears of sadness, tiredness, humiliation and hunger back. She would not cry in front of this pretentious boor.

He raised an eyebrow and clapped his hands together in mocking applause. "Very well done indeed, I've seldom seen better acting in Drury Lane! However, I have the proof here..." He took a piece of paper from his pocket and making a great show, he unfolded it and laid it on the desk in front of her. Smoothing it out with his hand, he gestured for her to look.

Keziah moved the lamp closer and taking the opportunity to surreptitiously wipe the tears from her eyes, she struggled to bring the words into focus. When she'd finished reading, she looked up at the young man. "And you think this is my work?" she asked, scornfully.

He blinked at her as if having been caught off-guard but if that was indeed so, he recovered himself quickly and added with certainty, "I do, indeed."

"Then, pray, allow me," she said, her anger now white-hot but at least the tears had gone. She took a sheet of paper from the drawer and dipping her pen in the ink she wrote in beautiful copperplate script:

*My name is Keziah Bonner.*
*I am the acting schoolmistress, not a blackmailer and I know how to spell Guineas.*

She spun the paper around so he could read it and crossed her arms, coldly watching his expression.

Silently he compared the crude, ill-formed letters and spelling errors on the folded piece of paper against the exquisite lettering that was still drying on the sheet Keziah had slid towards him.

Noting his confusion, she stood. "Now, if you'd excuse me please, sir, I have finally finished my work for the day and I'd like to go home." Picking up the lamp, she made to walk around him towards the door but he held out a restraining arm.

"I... I believe I may owe you an apology, Miss Bonner. I sincerely beg your pardon." His earlier haughtiness had gone and his expression was one of confusion and dismay. He ran his fingers through his fringe pushing it off his forehead. "It appears I was mistaken..."

"Indeed, you were," she replied coldly, "now, please allow me to pass."

"Wait!" Then in a gentler tone, he added, "please." He let his arm fall. "I must ask a favour of you. I humbly beg you to keep this information to yourself."

"Of course." said Keziah sharply, "I have no interest in this matter."

"Then, perhaps I could prevail upon you to help me..."

"Help you! I thought, sir, you'd made it very clear you had everything in hand. Didn't you say your uncle has influential friends? It's well known the village constable will do anything he asks. Surely, you need their assistance and not someone who, according to you, has very little presence – and someone who might be compared to a common actress!"

She'd gone too far. But what did it matter? She'd been foolish to believe Fortune would ever allow her to take control of her life. Her carefully laid plans and hard work were never going to come to anything. And now she'd destroyed any chance she'd had of advancing herself. All she had was the satisfaction of knowing for the first time in years, she'd spoken her mind. But she had no doubt she and Henry would live to regret this outburst.

However, to her surprise, he was silent and as she searched his face for rage or spite or some other understandable emotion, she simply saw uncertainty. His Adam's apple rose and fell several times and almost imperceptibly, he bit his lower lip. Finally, he sighed as if having come to a decision.

"Miss Bonner, I wonder if it would be possible for us to start again. Let us pretend I did not come in here accusing you, but merely to pay my respects. Of course, I know you will not be able to forget what was written in the letter but I hope you can forgive – if you cannot forget – my behaviour."

He searched her face but other than a slight frown at this unexpected turn in events, she said nothing.

He continued, "How do you do, Miss Bonner? Please allow me to introduce myself. My name is Matthew Gregory..." he gave a slight nod of greeting, "and I am trying to protect my little sister. I wonder if you can forgive my unforgivable rudeness?"

"Well, Mr Gregory, it happens that I have a younger brother who I would do anything to protect, so I understand your concern. However, I know nothing about the demand for fifty guineas for silence. Since your uncle owns everything in this valley, he must surely be able to deal with this. I fail to see how I can possibly help you."

He slowly shook his head. "My uncle doesn't know about this and it will be disaster if he finds out. It is a delicate matter and the fewer who know the better it will be for my sister."

"I see, so your threat to ruin my reputation, my livelihood and my home was an empty one?" The audacity of the man! She expected him to appear contrite but instead, a slow, mischievous smile spread across his face. It was the sort of smile that demanded a similar response and against her better judgement, she found she was smiling too. He obviously knew he'd been caught out and had chosen to find the humour and not the indignation.

Their smiles continued, as if they were co-conspirators in some secret venture and as she looked into his face, she noticed the deep, velvet-brown of his eyes which before, had glittered angrily but now looked at her in such a way, it was as if he was actually *seeing* her. Not just as an apprentice mill girl who needed to be supervised and managed – but as a person. And as a person who mattered.

She had never met a man like this. In her seventeen years, the males in her life had either been much older figures of authority or children such as the ones she taught at school. She'd had no reason to interact with anyone closer to her age or slightly older – in the workhouse, she'd been kept away from the men and boys, and here in Linderbourne, there had been little time or opportunity. No one she'd met before had taken the time to look at her like that, with a smile that had lit something deep inside from which warmth was radiating. And when he swept the fringe from his face, the heat intensified creeping up to her cheeks.

Embarrassed, she glanced away and busied herself tidying the pile of books that was already neatly arranged on the desk. She could easily match his anger and hurl his accusations back in his face. Even match his graciousness and accept his politeness. But this, whatever *this* was, she had no words to describe and she recognised she was in danger of making herself appear most foolish.

"It seems, Miss Bonner, I have no more clues and I wonder if you perhaps saw anyone else who might have stumbled across my sister and... and the other er... person."

"I?"

"Yes, my sister assures me you saw her... er... in the woods. We came to the mill earlier expressly for her to identify you. She pointed you out to me and then I said I would er... persuade you against this folly." He pointed at the letter.

Now, all was clear. Keziah had given no further thought to the lovers in the woods. Her life was complicated enough. So, that was why Matthew Gregory had stormed in and tried to intimidate her. She gave an understanding nod – after all, she knew the frustration and helplessness as one stood by and watched a loved one behave rashly, the consequences could be disastrous. She was certain she could do nothing to help Mr Gregory, but if there was anything that could be done, she would try. There was no doubt he wouldn't lift a finger to help her or Henry but that was no reason not to lend a hand to him and his sister. The world would be a darker place if everyone refused to perform an act of kindness because they stood to receive nothing in return. And it would give her a few more minutes with this exciting man before he realised she could do nothing for him and swept out as swiftly as he'd entered.

"Perhaps we might determine whose writing this is..." suggested Keziah with a confidence she didn't feel. "The most likely person is the er... gentleman in question."

"He was no gentleman, I assure you. Apparently, he's one of my uncle's carpenters."

Keziah looked up at the dusty beams of the schoolroom trying to visualise the scene she'd witnessed. As soon as she'd realised what was going on, she'd glanced away and she hadn't seen the man's face. But, if he was a carpenter, there were only two young men who it could have been and one of those had been sick for the past few weeks.

"Would the man be Tom Osgood?" she asked.

"My sister said he was called Tom, so yes, I suppose it must be. But she assures me he wouldn't have written such a letter."

"Probably not," she said thoughtfully, "but his brother may well have done."

"Do you know the brother?"

"Oh, yes!" Keziah said, unable to prevent her lip curling in scorn. "I know him very well. John Osgood. The overlooker in charge of the floor where my brother, Henry and I work."

"You don't like the man?"

"I should prefer to say the man does not like Henry or me."

"Is he capable of something like this?"

"I'm afraid I can't say." She must be careful. Mr Osgood worked for Mr Gregory's uncle. It wouldn't do to make accusations.

"But you don't trust him?"

"No, not in the slightest. He's a man who delights in tormenting apprentices but whether he would dare do this, I simply don't know."

As she'd been speaking, he'd moved around the desk until he was next to her and he turned the letter so they could both see it.

She wrapped her arms over her chest, trying to control her breathing which had speeded up as his arm brushed hers. He was so close, the scent of sandalwood filled her nostrils and she fervently hoped he couldn't smell the rancid oil they used in the mill which clung to everyone who worked there, despite her efforts to wash repeatedly. It was a stench that was now so familiar to her, she suspected she could no longer detect it even if it was there. However, he didn't draw away, indeed, he put his head closer to hers as they both peered at the letter.

"Do you think you could find a sample of Osgood's writing?" His words whisper-brushed her cheek and it seemed his face was turned towards hers and no longer looking at the letter.

She kept her gaze on the paper, pretending not to have noticed and struggled to keep her voice steady, hoping when she spoke, she wouldn't squeak. "I don't believe Mr Osgood has cause to write at work, I'm afraid. But I will keep my eyes open." She pushed the letter towards him to indicate he should take it and move away from her. But if he recognised he was being dismissed, he didn't move.

Finally, however, he reached out to take it. How beautiful his hand was, with long fingers that ended in perfect, clean nails. So, unlike everyone else in her world whose nails were grimy and whose skin was ingrained with dirt. The sight of him delicately placing one fingertip on the page and slowly sliding the paper towards him stoked the warm glow deep inside her once again.

"That would be most kind, Miss Bonner," he said and she swallowed as his words glided silkily across her cheek.

This, whatever it was, must stop. In the unlikely event Miss Maynard appeared now at the door she would not be happy to see her monitress so close to a man.

Stepping away from him, she said in the most neutral tone she could muster,

"If you would please excuse me, it's late. I must return to the Apprentice House."

"Of course," he said, "please forgive me for delaying you. Do you have far to ride?"

"Ride?" She frowned.

"Forgive me. I assume from your reply the Apprentice House must be close and there is no need to ride? I'm afraid I've only been staying with my uncle for a few days, so I'm not yet acquainted with the village. If you're walking home, I hope you'll allow me to escort you."

"That will not be necessary, thank you, Mr Gregory," she said half-alarmed at the thought of spending more time with him and half-elated.

"Nonsense I insist."

Once outside, he untied his horse and walked along by her side commenting on how lucky they were the spring rains had finally stopped and telling her about a recent outing to the theatre when there'd been a leak in the roof over the stage and the actors had humorously incorporated the bowl and drips into their dialogue. They'd walked about a hundred yards and rounded the first bend in the road, when Matthew glanced about and his voice took on a puzzled tone. "When you said the Apprentice House was nearby, Miss Bonner, I assumed you meant somewhere in the village. This road, well, if you can call it that, leads out of the village."

"The Apprentice House is still some way further off, Mr Gregory, but having accompanied me this far, I'm quite happy for you to leave me here and continue on your way."

"How far would you say it is from the school?"

"About half a mile." It was probably slightly further but she'd never really thought about it before. It was irrelevant. The distance had to be walked however long it was.

When he said, "I see…" she felt sure he'd turn back.

Her unreasonable disappointment mingled with relief. He'd said he was unfamiliar with the layout of the village and his comments thus far had demonstrated he'd offered to escort her home with no idea of how far out of his way it would take him.

"If it's so far, Miss Bonner, I will definitely accompany you. I cannot believe you would attempt to walk this far on your own in the dark."

She was glad of the darkness which hid her smile and the timely whinny of the horse that masked the laugh she'd not been able to stifle. But how foolish she'd feel when he finally discovered how far he would have to walk. Would he believe she'd been deceitful in not making it clear what his act of gallantry would cost him? Probably. And the thought he would resent her was uncomfortable.

"Pray, return home, Mr Gregory. I assure you, I'm used to this walk at night."

He was silent for a few moments as they continued, accompanied by the gentle thud of the horse's hooves and the nocturnal sounds of the forest.

"Am I to understand you walk home on your own like this every night?"

"On the evenings when I help out at the school, so, at the moment, yes."

She told him about standing in for Miss Maynard and how important it was for her to do a good job because her hope of one day becoming a schoolmistress rested on her success.

When she stopped speaking, he remained silent.

*Fool!* Her desire to show him she wasn't merely a drab who would be content to serve others with no thought of the future had driven her to confide too much in a stranger who couldn't possibly be interested in her. His comment about her journey home in the dark had simply shown how far removed his life was from hers. He would have servants, of course, and he'd be aware their lot was vastly different to his privileged circumstances. It wasn't that he didn't know, it was that he wouldn't care. And now, she'd poured out her dreams to his indifference.

Finally, they reached the Apprentice House.

"I hope your wishes come true, Miss Bonner." His voice lacked sincerity as if his mind was on something completely different. Then, nodding politely, he wished her goodnight.

On reaching the dormitory, Keziah crept to the window and looked down onto the road. The scene of such embarrassment. To her surprise, Mr Gregory was still there, astride his horse. In the moonlight, she could see his face turned towards the Apprentice House although he was too far away to read his expression. He waited several minutes more, then slowly turned the horse and was soon swallowed by the night.

Lucy was waiting for her brother in the entrance hall, hidden behind one of the grand, marble pillars. "Where have you been?" Her eyes were wild, "Uncle Obadiah's not happy. I told him you were familiarising yourself with the area but you went out hours ago. It's pitch black now!'

"I had to wait until everyone had left the schoolhouse before I could approach the girl, I could hardly stroll in during a lesson and confront her, could I?"

"Well, no, I suppose not... Anyway, what happened? Will she withdraw her threat? Did you have to pay her?"

He held up his hand to silence her. "I'm sorry, Lucy, but it wasn't her."

"Of course, it was! Her face is imprinted in my memory."

"No, I mean she saw you... but she's not the person who sent the letter."

"But she must be!" Lucy stamped her foot. "The trouble with you, Matthew, is you can so easily be swayed by a pretty face!"

"I tell you, it wasn't her, Luce. She showed me a sample of her writing and whatever you may think, it definitely wasn't her."

Lucy groaned. "So now somebody else knows!"

"I understand your frustration, Lucy, but there was no other way of finding out whether it was her. I thought I could exert a little pressure and hoped that would be enough for her to change her mind. But she didn't know what I was talking about. I had to show her the letter and her writing is completely different—"

"You showed her the letter?" Lucy's voice rose in pitch and volume. It echoed around the hall, shocking them both into silence as they held their breath and waited to see if anyone would come to find out what was happening. No one came.

"I had better go and beg our uncle's pardon," Matthew whispered.

Lucy nodded and after another glance left and right to ensure the brother and sister were unobserved, she tiptoed upstairs to her bedroom.

The conversation with his uncle would need to be handled with the utmost care. He'd already displeased Uncle Obadiah by having run up huge debts at his club which his uncle had paid after extracting a promise of self-restraint. Unfortunately, one particularly large wager had not gone Matthew's way. His friend, Lord Sparham, owed him a large sum but until he repaid his debt, Matthew didn't have enough to cover what he owed. Life in London was expensive. But unfortunately, Uncle Obadiah, with his businessman's knowledge knew exactly how expensive and exactly how extravagant Matthew had been. Nevertheless, so far Uncle Obadiah had covered all his debts.

Matthew wished for a large glass of fortifying brandy as he knocked on his uncle's library door but perhaps it was best he didn't smell of alcohol. That wouldn't please his abstemious uncle at all.

"Enter!"

Matthew took a deep breath, arranged his features into what he hoped was his most contrite and charming face, and entered the library.

Uncle Obadiah was sitting in his favourite chair next to the fire. "You lost your way?" His eyes opened in surprise. "What were you doing out in the first place, Matthew? You know your aunt wanted us to dine together."

"I beg your pardon, Uncle, and I will of course make my apologies to Aunt Hannah. I merely intended to explore the village but I'm afraid I mistook the way."

"But, Matthew, you could walk through the village in five minutes. You were on horseback; how could you possibly have got lost?"

"When I got to the crossroads, I thought I'd found a shortcut but it turned out not to be so."

"Did you take the road towards the Apprentice House?"

"I believe I must have. About half a mile from the village, I came across a large house and then the road narrowed considerably, so I thought I'd better return."

"But to get to Linderbourne Hall, you have to go uphill. The road you're describing runs along the valley. How could you not have noticed?"

"I... I must have become disorientated in the dark..." The conversation wasn't going well. It was too unbelievable. Then Matthew added, "and then Diablo stepped on something in the dark and I had to dismount and lead him home." This wasn't true but Matthew gambled that his uncle, settled in his library at the back of the mansion, would not have seen him ride to the stables and leave the horse with the grooms. Finally, Uncle Obadiah seemed satisfied until a thought occurred to him.

"And what were you looking for in the village? You understand almost everyone living there works for me. We are very careful to keep... disreputable... er... people out."

Matthew suppressed a smile. By 'people', he guessed his uncle meant 'women' but he pretended not to understand. "I wasn't looking for anyone in particular," he said aware that was exactly what he'd been doing, but not for the reason his uncle suspected. "I'm keen to find my way about." Uncle Obadiah regarded him over his clay pipe with raised, unbelieving eyebrows. Matthew continued, "because I would like to take a greater interest in the mill and how it works."

A masterstroke! That caught Uncle Obadiah's attention! And it was partially true, but again, not for the reasons his uncle would have wanted.

"Well, that gladdens my heart, Matthew! You have no idea how long I've waited to hear you say you were taking an interest in something... other than the things a young man would usually have put to one side by your age."

Matthew remembered countless other conversations with his uncle where he'd felt remorse and shame for his reckless extravagance. He'd promised to reform, even meaning it from time to time, but now, on seeing his uncle's pleasure, his guilt was an almost solid thing, weighing like lead in his stomach. For the first time, his uncle's face held hope. This was even more poignant because although the elder man had earned a fortune from his mill and other business endeavours, he would never be considered a gentleman. Nor would his wife be seen as a lady. Perhaps one day, Matthew's cousins might be accepted into society and their wealth would be enough to gain them admittance but not quite yet. It was ironic because Aunt Hannah was Sir Hugh's sister, and as such, she had a position in society. Or, more accurately, she'd once had a position in society. Once, Hannah Gregory had been seen at all the best London social events but she'd fallen in love and married a man, who although not low-born, had gone into business and worked for a living. After that, she discovered many doors closed to her. She never complained but Matthew suspected it still irritated and saddened her, despite the fact she had a more costly collection of gowns and jewels than many of the women of the upper class with whom she'd once mixed. Although, he knew, gowns and jewels were only of value when you could show them off at sumptuous soirées.

But Uncle Obadiah's vast fortune had been put to more beneficial use than to simply adorn his wife – he was also supporting his brother-in-law, as well as Sir Hugh's family, his London house and country estates.

Matthew's cheeks glowed with shame and he shifted from one foot to the other. His lie had prompted the frank and almost boyishly eager expression of his uncle, on hearing of his nephew's interest in the business. Would it hurt to take an interest in what this remarkable man had achieved? Perhaps he ought to take note. Perhaps he owed his uncle. He had no other plan for his life.

Plan. That fascinating schoolmistress had spoken of a plan in a voice so passionate, he'd been surprised when she'd finished speaking. She'd told him about becoming a teacher and finding a cottage such as the humble dwellings in the village where she could look after her brother. It was such a meagre aspiration and yet she spoke as if it would lift her far above her current position. Could her life be that bad? His uncle employed her and gave her food and lodging. She was surely one of the fortunate ones?

"And what would you like to know about the mill?" Uncle Obadiah asked. He was sitting upright now, alert and ready to talk about his beloved business. "Sit, sit." He motioned to the chair opposite. "I expect you'd like to know about the waterwheel and the mechanism for driving the shafts..."

Matthew would rather have known about the conditions under which the employees worked but once his uncle had started, he thought it best not to interrupt. At least while he was learning about water flow rates, the new headrace and tailrace and the number of machines in the mill, his uncle was not asking for details about his gambling debts. That would undoubtedly come on the morrow.

Uncle Obadiah's detailed explanation about the differences between undershot and overshot waterwheels, angles, load, gravity and power had continued for some time and Matthew had followed all the details and felt he had a good idea of how the machines were driven.

But as soon as he climbed into bed, the powerful waterwheel that drove the axles, belts and shafts had been forgotten. They had not filled his dreams. It was the young schoolmistress, Keziah Bonner, who had done that. She wasn't the most beautiful girl he'd ever met but she was certainly the most alluring... and the most perplexing.

In the past, he'd seen admiration, jealousy, flirtation and naked desire in the eyes of so many women but never before had anyone glared at him with such passion. True, it was passion borne out of anger and all of it had been directed at him, but its intensity had thrilled him. All the women he'd so far met, seemed pale and insignificant beside the fiery schoolmistress, like insipid watercolour figures next to a vibrant oil painting.

It had been the image of Keziah; her hands on her hips and her eyes glittering with such ferocity, that had filled his dreams and she was his first thought when he awoke.

Keziah Bonner. How delicious the name felt on his tongue. For months, he'd awoken to the taste of stale brandy but now, his mind was sharp, his mouth fresh and his yearning keen.

When Jefferson arrived with hot water and fresh towels, he informed Matthew his uncle had unexpectedly been called away to Nottingham early that morning and had taken his aunt, who had decided to go on a shopping trip with Lucy and her daughters. They would stay with friends and return the following morning.

He had a whole day to fill until he could go back to the schoolhouse after the children had gone, on the pretext of finding out if Keziah had discovered anything about John Osgood. Of course, it was information he needed if he was to help his sister before Saturday when the letter had directed her to take fifty guineas to the churchyard. Matthew had three days to decide what to do.

Once Jefferson had finished dressing him, he combed his long, dark hair, staring at this reflection in the looking-glass. Usually, he had a fondness for women with hair as blonde as his was dark but the previous evening, he'd been entranced by Keziah's rich, copper tints that glinted in the soft lamplight. He paused, staring into the mirror but instead of seeing his reflection, he saw her and pictured how her hair would look if he'd removed the pins that held it back so severely and allowed it to cascade over her shoulders. Despite having been tied back neatly, tendrils had escaped from their confines and he imagined how it would feel to wrap one around his finger, then to gently draw it down and to allow it to spring back into shape.

"Ahem!" Jefferson cleared his throat and Matthew was jolted back to the present. "Should I inform Cook you will be down for breakfast presently, sir?"

"Ah, yes! Yes! Thank you, Jefferson." He would take his time and while he ate, he'd read Uncle's London newspapers – no matter that they were days out of date, as they'd probably taken longer to reach Linderbourne than he had. He'd go for a stroll. Or a ride. Or sit...

The day stretched interminably before him. It was hours before it would be time to go to the schoolhouse. He consoled himself with the thought that being alone all day in the Hall, meant no one would worry about him not being there for dinner that evening when he intended to be out. And he would be able to walk Keziah home again. He would ask her to talk once again about her hopes for the future. How refreshing it was to hear about someone's plans. No matter that her aspirations were humble, what had entranced him was the way her voice had strengthened when she'd spoken about the future she'd imagined and yet, at the same time, it had softened. Foolishly, he'd said very little to her. He'd envied her sense of direction, wondering for the first time why he had none. And then, she'd left him in the darkness to stare at the forbidding building into which she'd slipped and to wish he'd delayed her longer.

Once he was seated at the table in the morning room, a young girl limped in with a pot of coffee.

Usually, he wouldn't have noticed her but he wanted to know more about the people in the mill. The previous evening, Matthew had tried to direct his uncle's attention to his employees but without success. When Matthew had questioned Jefferson earlier, he'd professed to know nothing of mills or the people who worked there. He'd been brought from London by Mr Rigby and spent all his time in the Hall, he informed Matthew, as if taking great pains to disassociate himself with such a dubious enterprise as "that clunking, clanking building."

Perhaps the young maid would know more. She said her name was Mary and she knew all about the mill as she'd once been an apprentice there until her accident. She looked down sadly at her legs.

"Me skirts got caught in the machine," she said making twirling gestures with her fingers that Matthew took to represent the shafts of the machinery, "And..." She left the sentence hanging but added, "the mill surgeon did a good job of mending me legs though. Then, when I could walk, Mr Rigby said I could work up here in the Hall. He's a nice man. And now, I don't ever 'ave to worry about creeping under them machines again."

"What were you doing under the machines?" Matthew asked in surprise.

"Why, cleaning the cotton off the floor, sir," she said as if it was obvious. "The overlookers like everything to be kept clean, so the smallest children are sent under the machines to sweep up. And that's when sometimes..." she twirled her fingers again to indicate the machinery turning.

Matthew knew that children were often employed to do difficult jobs. Didn't one read in the newspapers of the scandal of the chimney sweep boys who died in soot-filled flues? But people were beginning to speak out against such cruelty and soon, surely there'd be legislation preventing such deplorable practices.

But the thought that this small, pinch-faced girl had been tangled up in machinery in the mill was a shock. His uncle was a good man, so it must have been a freak accident, but his interest had prompted Mary to talk and she told him of fingers caught in moving parts and several horrific injuries that had occurred during her time in the mill. Even several deaths.

Matthew put his toast down. This was not the sort of thing he wanted to hear at breakfast. It was not the sort of thing he wanted to hear at all.

"But the mill is a good place to work is it not?" he asked. She'd surely exaggerated. Over time, there'd be accidents anywhere.

She stared at him in silence for a beat, then finally, said, "Yes, sir." But her voice lacked conviction.

"Mr Rigby is a good employer is he not?"

"Oh, yes, sir!" she said but her eyes darted left and right and she swallowed as if she'd said too much.

He smiled at her. "And yet?"

Mary looked like a startled rabbit, "Well, sir, it's just that although Mr Rigby is a fine man... his overlookers are not. They like to pick on people... especially the children."

"But surely the overlookers must do as my uncle tells them?"

"I suppose, sir. But Mr Rigby is never there when they beat us."

"Beat you?" No, surely not in his uncle's mill. Elsewhere, in other parts of the country, perhaps, but not in Linderbourne.

Matthew had heard enough. Perhaps the girl's accident had addled her wits. This was not what he'd expected at all and yet the name John Osgood had provoked a remarkable change in Keziah's expression too and he considered for the first time that people were being mistreated not a mile away in his uncle's mill.

Matthew pushed the toast away. His stomach churned. He wouldn't be able to eat with all the images the girl had raised, fresh in his mind. He'd spent so many years perfecting an air of careless indifference to his father's coldness, that he realised he'd come to believe it himself. It was as if he wore spectacles that didn't make the world clearer but did quite the opposite, blurring what was really there and effectively deadening all feeling. He'd filled his life with amusing people with whom he'd spent diverting evenings betting obscenely large sums of money on foolish wagers, merely for the few moments of thrill before the outcome was revealed. He'd drunk to excess, to deaden the pain of his father's rejection and he'd surrounded himself with reputable and disreputable women in an effort to forget everything. It seemed to have worked. He'd lost touch with real life, but now as this small girl – still a child – limped back to the kitchen with the remains of his breakfast, it was as if the spectacles had reversed and everything was now coming clearly into focus. A focus so sharp, it was painful to look at.

The previous evening, he'd hinted to his uncle he would take an interest in the business in the future without truly meaning it. The lie had slipped easily from his tongue. After all, he was a gentleman, and gentlemen did not go into business. But now, he was beginning to wonder if he ought to find out more about what happened to put toast on his plate. And not only toast... his uncle's fortune paid for only the finest food and wine.

One day, he would become Sir Matthew Gregory and he would need to ensure he had sufficient funds to manage the family's estates. He knew of many gentlemen who lived beyond their means, several families had fallen on hard times and were no longer able to mix in London society. His friend, Felix, the new Lord Sparham, for example, currently owed a fortune and he was struggling to continue with his extravagant lifestyle.

It seemed to Matthew, there were several options. Many in his position sought a wealthy heiress to marry but Matthew refused to even consider that solution. He was in no rush to marry and the thought of using a woman to finance his family was abhorrent.

Another possibility was to carry on living the life of a gentleman and relying on his uncle's generosity to pay for all expenses, in which case, he faced the prospect that one day, Uncle Obadiah might refuse further payment. Then Matthew would not be able to afford to take part in London society.

The last option was to earn money of his own. Although he'd studied Law, he had no plans to become a lawyer, but it would be an enormous step to involve himself in lowly commerce such as Linderbourne Mill.

And once he'd taken that decision, there would be no going back. London society would neither forgive nor forget.

Without funds, he would eventually be denied his place amongst the elite. But if he joined Uncle Obadiah, perhaps one day, people would be more accepting of gentlemen going into business.

He would consider the possibility and while he did so, he'd discover more about the conditions of the mill workers. If anything needed reforming, then he'd find out and act on their behalf.

It appeared he had much to learn. He'd asked Mary how long it would be before the employees arrived at the mill, imagining Keziah strolling through the morning sunshine to work.

Mary had smiled as if he'd been jesting before she realised his question had been serious. "Why, sir, they've been there four and a half hours already." The she told him they worked more than twelve hours every day except Sunday. Could that possibly be true?

He decided he'd send to the mill for Keziah, pretending his uncle had need of her and at least she'd have a pleasant afternoon away from work before she started at the schoolhouse. And he would have the pleasure of her company.

The day had brightened considerably.


"You!" said Mr Osgood, pointing at Keziah with his stubby finger. "You're wanted up at the Hall. Get moving!"

Fear shot through her. Why would Mr Rigby send for her? In a panic, she glanced about, looking for Henry but he was at the other end of the room. Had someone reported him? But if so, why not send for Henry and Jack? No, this was something to do with her. Another thought occurred to her – perhaps it wasn't Mr Rigby who'd called for her but his wife. After all, she took an interest in the school. Did she want to tell Keziah her services were no longer required? But surely, she would write a letter? She wouldn't allow herself to even consider the possibility her work was not satisfactory and she was being let go. That couldn't be possible, she worked too hard for that. Unless, of course, Matthew Gregory had somehow let Osgood know she'd pointed the finger at him... If that was the case, she was surely in trouble.

Her head spun with possibilities – none of them favourable.

She wiped her hands on her apron and when Mr Osgood unlocked the door she slipped through, hardly reaching the top of the stairs before she heard the clanging of the keys as he locked it behind her. Once outside, she gratefully sucked in mouthfuls of the clean, fresh air and glanced at the clock tower. By the time she walked to and from the Hall – assuming, of course, she wasn't being dismissed – dinner time would be over and she'd be locked out of Osgood's room for the rest of the afternoon. And that meant she'd have to make up the time and would be late to start school.

A stone or something sharp in her boot had worked its way under her heel but she dared not stop to remove it and as she hurried along, she tried her best to tuck wisps of hair back into place and to brush away the cotton fluff.

She wanted to look presentable.

But for whom? Mr Rigby? Mrs Rigby? Her mind flitted from one to the other as she weighed up which of the two people who controlled her world could cause her the most pain. The only certainty was that there appeared to be no good reason for either of them to summon her to their home.

She arrived at the sweeping semi-circular drive in front of the mansion out of breath and aware that her earlier attempts to tidy her hair had been undone by the wind. A man was leaning with arms crossed against one of the pillars that stood on either side of the enormous front door and on catching sight of her, he straightened and ran down the steps. He was dressed elegantly in dark blue and grey and with disbelief, she saw it was Matthew Gregory.

He waited at the bottom of the steps and smiled when she reached him. Had his uncle sent him to meet her?

"Good morning, Miss Bonner," he said, his smile suggesting they were sharing a secret. And yet it was a secret about which she knew nothing. Her eyes flicked upwards and seeing the height of the sun, she frowned slightly but didn't add, 'It's hardly morning, sir, and I know this for certain because currently, I should be eating dinner – a meal I will now miss.'

Instead, she nodded as curtly as politeness would allow. He appeared not to notice her reserve and beckoned to her to follow him as he bounded up the stairs to the front door. She hesitated knowing she should present herself at the rear of the house at the servants' entrance but he looked back when he reached the top step and seeing her hesitation, he said, "Come! No one is home except me and I have no intention of going to the back of the Hall when there are perfectly serviceable doors here."

Then, assuming she would follow him as he'd instructed, he entered through the doors, leaving them open to reveal a stunning entrance hall.

No one was home? How could that be? And if that was the case, who had summoned her? Surely Matthew Gregory had not called her away from her work simply to ask about John Osgood? But she suspected he was selfish enough to have done just that. He'd be worried about his sister and not care she'd have to make up every minute she wasn't at work.

She hurried across the black and white marble floor wondering whether she was leaving behind crumbs of mud she'd picked up on her walk up the hill. How embarrassing if she had left a trail.

Matthew held the door open to a large, bright room and as she entered, he indicated she should sit at the mahogany table on one of the maroon velvet-covered chairs. He tugged twice on the ornate bell-pull next to the fireplace and by the time he'd taken a seat opposite, a small, thin girl who Keziah thought she recognised, appeared from a much smaller door in the corner carrying a tray. When she saw the young girl's limp, Keziah remembered her as having been involved in an accident in the mill several years before.

The girl's lips squeezed tightly together with the effort of carrying the tray and contents safely to the table and finally, she allowed herself a glimmer of a smile as she successfully placed everything on a linen mat on the polished mahogany.

When Keziah realised the coffee pot, cups, saucers and plates of tiny biscuits the maid had placed on the table were intended for her and Matthew, her cheeks flared. What must this girl be thinking? If Matthew was correct and there were no other members of the family in the house yet he was entertaining a mill girl, then only one conclusion could be drawn. It was unlikely Matthew would care what a servant thought but Keziah knew she'd be judged harshly and if it got back to Miss Maynard...

Keziah sat rigidly on the edge of the chair until the girl had left and Matthew began to pour out coffee for them.

"I've been summoned to see either the master or mistress, so if neither of them is here, then I must return immediately." She stood and he smiled up at her making a placatory gesture with his hand.

"No, no! It is I who called you." He smiled conspiratorially. "I thought perhaps you could let me know if you had any news about John Osgood and—"

Before he could finish she leapt up and stepped away from him, her eyes wide. Her mouth was open but she was so enraged no sound came out. She simply turned her hands palms up, as if to ask how he could be so overwhelmingly foolish. Finally, she found her voice. "You called me away from my work to ask me about that man?"

"Well... yes," he said, his earlier confident tone gone, "I thought you'd appreciate some time away from work. I'd planned to show you the garden. The weather is most pleasant."

Keziah shook her head in disbelief. "Time away from work? There is no such thing for me! I must make up every second I'm away from the mill. Thanks to you, I've missed my dinner and will not eat again until about ten o'clock. And far worse than that – I have no idea how I'm going to be able to make up this time and carry out my duties as a schoolmistress today... if indeed, with my reputation in ruins, I am allowed to do so." At the thought of that, a lump grew in her throat and she was unable to continue.

He said nothing but his expression was one of surprise and hurt and she realised he'd no idea of the repercussions for her. Indeed, he'd treated her like a lady. But she wasn't a lady. This was his world and he had no business meddling in hers. He'd not only cause dreadful problems for her at work, but he may also have compromised her reputation.

"I must go." She turned towards the door.

"No, wait! Once again, Miss Bonner, I need to beg your pardon and I will try to make amends. I admit, I deliberately made it sound as though my uncle required you here but only Mary knows you've come. She'll say nothing – I'll make sure of that. But as for you making up time at work, I confess I didn't know. I will order the gig to be brought to the front of the house and I'll drive you back, so at least there will be less time to make up.

"And what will happen when people see me return with you in your gig? Thank you but no thank you. I must go."

As she retraced her steps across the tiled floor of the entrance hall, towards the large door, she realised she probably should have used the servants' entrance but there was no time now and opening one of the doors she ran outside. At least she hadn't left a trail of mud when she'd entered. There would be no sign she'd ever been.

When she arrived back at the mill, she discovered there'd been an accident. She held her breath praying it hadn't involved Henry, but for once, the worst had not happened and she discovered Mr Osgood had slipped on some oil and had fallen, hitting his head. He had only been bruised and dazed and the mill surgeon was attending him. There'd be repercussions, that was certain. Osgood would demand someone paid and that person would most likely be one of the people on whom he normally picked, but Keziah had not been there so she couldn't be blamed.

Later, when she caught up with Henry, he said he'd been at the far end of the room and nowhere near where the oil had been spilt. Mr

Wilson, the kindest of the overlookers supervised the cleaning up of the spillage, which meant the door was unlocked when Keziah arrived back at the mill, hot and dishevelled, and she managed to slip in without anyone noticing.

Mr Osgood had gone home and Mr Wilson, knowing Keziah had permission to leave early so she could fulfil her teaching duties, allowed her to go. So, despite being ravenously hungry and her boots rubbing her heels again after the long walk to and from the Hall, Matthew Gregory had not disrupted her life too much. One thing was certain. He wouldn't seek her out again. She wondered what he'd do about the blackmail demand. He would need to take some action before Saturday which was only two days hence. But there was nothing she could do for him. Life was too precarious for her to be able to worry about anyone other than Henry.

After Keziah had marched out of the morning room, Matthew poured himself a cup of coffee and slowly sipped the hot, pungent liquid. His first thought had been to run after her but he suspected he'd only make things worse. He'd not intended to cause Keziah so many problems. On the contrary, he'd wanted to do something pleasant for her. Well, yes, he admitted to himself, mostly he wanted to do something pleasant for himself; to avoid the silence of the echoing house, to fill the empty hours. He'd longed to allow his eyes to feast on her remarkable face and trim figure. And then who knew what might happen? Of course, he knew exactly what would definitely not happen. She was a captivating blend of innocence and... What? He couldn't define it... certainly, she was not experienced with men, he felt sure of that, and yet neither was she ignorant. Aware but wary... A fascinating mixture. She was a conundrum and he'd seen enough of her to know he longed to find out more.

Having upset her twice, he must try to make it up to her. He summoned Mary and when she arrived, he said, "Clear this away, please and inform Cook I will require a light supper this evening and that she is to prepare a large cake, bread, ham, cheese and a dozen or so apples. I'd like everything packed in a basket, to be ready for me as soon as possible."

There was nothing he could do to put right the harm he'd caused, but he could ensure Keziah didn't go hungry that evening. However, he'd realised the utmost care would be required. There must be no risk of anyone discovering he'd sent her a gift for fear his gesture might be misconstrued and threaten her reputation. And he suspected she wouldn't accept something she might consider to be charity. After some thought, he'd decided to send a gift to the school for the children... and the teacher. It would look as though it had been his aunt's idea and although Keziah would know the truth, she could hardly turn the food away.

As for the time she'd have to make up, there was nothing he could do about that but he would also go down to the school before anyone arrived and put the basket inside, then when the children came, he'd ensure they waited quietly until Keziah was released from work. Miss Maynard, nor anyone else, would have cause for complaint.

He felt satisfied he would have gone some way towards making things up to Keziah, and the bottomless chasm of empty hours that had lain before him could now be crossed with one large leap.

But first, there was the problem of Lucy's blackmailer and he must concentrate on that. While he waited for cakes to bake and food to appear, he would turn his mind to that.

Thanks to Mr Osgood's accident and Mr Wilson's leniency, Keziah had time to go home, wash and change in the Apprentice House, and arrive at the schoolhouse at the normal time. She stopped abruptly as she entered the room, having detected something was wrong.

No, not wrong, exactly – just different.

Memories of her childhood flooded into her mind. Sitting at the table in the dining room above her father's watchmakers' shop with her mother and Eva; their servant, Sarah, placing dishes of delicious food in front of them and the warmth of the fire in the hearth. Henry had yet to be born in that far off glimpse of what felt like a different life. Keziah screwed her eyes up tightly, trying to preserve the image of her family together enjoying each other's company and the good food that Sarah had placed before them. It was so vivid, she could smell the sweet, spicy aroma that had filled the room so many years ago. Tears filled her eyes as the harder she tried to hold on to the picture, the more it seemed to shift and evaporate, even though the smell was lingering.

No, not lingering, the smell was growing stronger.

And then she noticed the basket. Had Miss Maynard left something for the children? Keziah lifted the cloth that covered the contents and released more of the delicious aroma of what she could now see was a large cake. And at the other end of the basket, were bread, cheese, ham and apples packed carefully so as not to bruise them. Tucked down the side of the cake was a note.

*For the children and to make up for your lost dinner, M.*

She snatched the note up and folding it, tucked it in her pocket. It wouldn't do for anyone to know that Mr Rigby's nephew had sent her a present. But the gift, as kindly as she was sure it was meant, would now cause her problems for she could hardly carry on with the lessons while the children were eating and she knew from their chattering voices, they had already gathered outside the door, she wouldn't be able to hide the food either, for the room was filled with its delicious aroma. To expect hungry children who'd been working all day to study, while they were being tantalised by the sweet smells was simply asking for trouble. She had been given food for them and she would share it out. There was no choice in the matter.

There was very little learning done that evening in the festive atmosphere and Keziah hoped they would still have sufficient hunger to eat the unappetising supper they'd be served when they got back to the Apprentice House or questions would be asked. She'd told them it was a gift about which they should say nothing and each child had understood. The apprentices knew that extra food was to be eaten quickly, enjoyed if possible, but never discussed. It was unlikely to be approved by the authorities, having most likely been stolen or acquired in some other manner that ought not be divulged.

The children were in high spirits when they left the schoolhouse and for the first time, Keziah was glad to see them go. The whole lesson had been slightly out of her control and now with a sinking heart she looked around the schoolroom – there were crumbs everywhere. She hadn't realised how dirty the floor was until it was time for them to leave. She'd considered holding them back to clean up but if they'd all returned to the Apprentice House late, questions would be asked. She wished she'd thought of it earlier but she'd been more concerned with keeping the noise levels down. With a sigh, she fetched the broom, and starting at one end of the room she began to sweep. Keziah reconciled herself to a late night.

She hadn't got far when the door opened and Matthew Gregory stood there with what appeared to be a self-satisfied smile upon his face as if waiting for some sign from her that she was grateful.

*Let him wait!*

Coldly, she looked up and leaning the broom against the nearest table, she put her hands on her hips and said, "I believe it is you I have to thank for the basket of food. I am grateful but please in future keep away from me and do not send any more gifts. I understand you need to know about John Osgood but sadly I have nothing to tell you. Please, I beg you, keep away. You cause me nothing but problems—"

"Problems?" His face fell and his lips formed the beginning of the word 'Why?' but no sound came from his mouth.

He genuinely had no idea.

"This!" she said crossly flinging her arms wide to indicate the floor, "I've had to maintain control of a group of excited children many of whom have never seen so much food, much less eaten so well. I have been able to teach them nothing and I would be very surprised if no one passed by and heard the uproar and have informed Miss Maynard. And now I have all this to clean..."

"I... I did not think."

"And that is why I beg you, please, keep away from me. You always bring trouble." Her heart sank, knowing her harsh words had resulted in his pained expression. He meant well. But he must stop. Eventually, he'd do something that would cause her downfall.

"No!" he said, "I can put this right. I'll help you clear up and afterwards, I'll drive you home in the gig – No, wait!" He held his hand up to stop her protest. "I'll stop before the Apprentice House for you to alight and walk home so no one will observe us. You see? I am learning."

His eagerness was touching. But tiredness and frustration after such a difficult day were dominating her thoughts. She had no idea why this man was trying so hard to please her. Perhaps it was simply that he needed her help to save his sister's reputation but she doubted it. She'd already told him she hadn't managed to find out anything and yet still he wanted to help her tidy and to take her home. Perversely, she realised, she wanted him there too and it wasn't simply that she wanted help to finish cleaning up.

He must have taken her silence as acceptance. "So," he said, seizing the broom she'd leaned against the table, "the sooner we sweep up, the sooner we go home."

She laughed at the way he held the broom. He must have seen people sweep but he obviously hadn't taken much notice. Judging by the way he gripped the handle, he'd never used one before and he looked up at her as if pleading for help.

"This looks harder than I thought it would be. I think I need a lesson," he said ruefully although she suspected he was feigning incompetence. Surely no one could be this awkward with a broom. Could they?

"Like this," she said taking the broom from him and showing him the best way of holding it. "Perhaps it would be faster if you moved the chairs while I sweep."

"No, I can't let a broom beat me," he said, "how would I ever live it down?" He smiled at her and she found it was becoming harder to remember how tiring and frustrating the day had been, and how she'd longed to go home.

She thought he'd changed his mind as he stepped past her until she realised he moved until he was behind her.

"I need a teacher..." he whispered, sliding his arms around her and placing his hands over hers on the broom handle, "to show me what to do in case a situation like this should arise in the future. And as you are the schoolmistress..."

She stiffened, knowing he had no interest in brooms or sweeping. However, although his chest lightly touched her shoulders as he reached around her, he did not press his body into her back. Instead, he held her like one might cradle a tiny, nervous bird, with a tender but gentle touch that would allow it to fly should it so wish. Her heart was pounding but she found to her surprise, she didn't wish to fly. She liked the warmth of his body against her back and the brush of his hair against hers and she wondered what it would feel like if his arms were to close about her and hold her tightly.

"I feel there should be more to it than this," he said, resting his chin on her shoulder with his face so close to hers, she wondered if he could feel the heat radiating from her cheek. "Shouldn't the broom be moving?"

"W...well... you just..." She demonstrated, aware of the strong muscles of his arms enclosing hers as she brushed the broom back and forth, back and forth. The motion was so ineffective, she knew without looking down, the floor would be no cleaner. However, as they moved together, as if dancing, she could feel his chest muscles rippling against her back and his cheek touch hers.

"It's much more interesting than I'd ever imagined. I feel I could sweep all night. But we don't appear to be moving very far."

She'd been aware that with his arms around her, she could hardly step backwards and press herself against him, nor pull him against her if she moved forwards.

"Perhaps that's enough for the first lesson?" She didn't want him to let go but they could hardly stand there much longer locked together in such an unseemly way. Even if he appeared to have enough respect for her not to press himself hard against her.

"Yes, I'll leave this to you and move the chairs as you suggested. Even I can't fail at that." She could hear the laughter in his voice and she suspected he knew the effect his closeness had on her.

"Yes, yes! Perhaps that would be best," she said, trying to keep her voice steady.

He trailed his middle fingers along the backs of her hands as far as her wrists and then, she was grateful he turned away and busied himself moving chairs – at least he couldn't see her blushing cheeks and neither could she see his expression. They both worked quickly and silently and by the time the floor was clean, Keziah's cheeks had cooled, although she still fancied she could feel the warmth of his body against her back and her nostrils were filled, not with the sweet, spicy smell of cake but with the woody fragrance of the sandalwood that subtly clung to his body.

He lifted a chair out of the way of her broom and looked at her with a quizzical expression, "Am I doing this correctly?" he asked with a mischievous grin, "only I seem to have got everything else I've done today wrong. Too high? Too low?" He tipped the chair to one side. "Too much of an angle?"

He smiled with delight that he'd made her laugh and as they worked together quickly through the room, the awkwardness between them dissipated.

"Does it meet your standards?" he asked when they'd finished. "I seem to have worked up quite an appetite." He lifted the cloth which was draped over the basket and peered inside. "There's nothing left. In fact, I think there was more food left on the floor."

"If you send a basket of food to a group of apprentice children, you must expect them to eat everything." She smiled at his rueful expression.

He continued peering into the empty basket. "Are you saying my uncle doesn't feed them enough?"

"No, I'm not saying that," she said slowly, "no one is starving but there's usually barely enough, so if a meal is missed—" She stopped abruptly and colour flooded her cheeks as she realised it might sound as though she were taking the opportunity to reproach him again for causing her to miss dinner; it seemed most ungracious after his generous act.

He'd obviously misinterpreted her inadvertent reminder, as he was now frowning.

"I... I didn't mean to criticise..." she said hurriedly but when he looked up at her, she could see he'd been thinking of something else entirely. Now his attention was back on her and the earlier light-hearted atmosphere had returned, "No, no of course not. Well," he said with a gentle smile, "if we're finished, Miss Bonner, please allow me to take you home."

To Keziah's surprise, she realised she was glancing around for something to delay them; for some excuse to spend a little longer with him. But there was nothing more to do.

He picked up the basket. "I expect you're keen to see me go." The slight downturn of the corners of his mouth suggested he was hurt, yet his eyes sparkled as if he was teasing her.

She wanted to share with him that this had been the best part of her day, despite having told him earlier she never wanted to see him again. But that would have been rather foolish and very unfair to him, to blow hot and cold.

Fair to him? Who was she trying to fool? What did he care if she froze solid or burst into flames? This was simply an hour's diversion, to keep him amused while his family was away. As soon as he'd dealt with his sister's problem, she wouldn't see him again. He'd go back to London and forget the night he'd played at being a servant and comically pretended to fail at the simplest tasks.

Keziah followed him out of the schoolhouse, across the bridge to where he had left the gig. She wondered if this had been thoughtfulness on his part to hide the fact he'd been in the schoolhouse, or because it had somehow suited him. But if it had suited him, she couldn't see how. It would have been far easier to have left the gig closer.

Mr Gregory helped her up and with a click of his tongue, urged the horse on, back across the bridge and turned left onto the road towards the Apprentice House.

He stopped the horse well before the Apprentice House and immediately jumped down to help her out. Was it ungrateful to wish he'd walked home with her like he had the previous night? It had been thoughtful of him to drive her but it was over so soon. He held out his hand to take hers and helped her onto the road but instead of letting it go, he placed his other hand over hers.

"Once again," he said, "I beg your pardon for all that happened today. I hope you understand I meant no harm. And I appreciate that you tried to find out something about John Osgood."

"But I failed to find anything useful."

"On the contrary. Before you told me he was Tom Osgood's brother, I had no idea who might be a suspect."

"But you are still not certain it is him."

"No, but I'm resigned to find out on Saturday night. Do you think he's too injured from his fall to keep the appointment?"

"I believe he'll be better by then. The surgeon thought him well enough to walk home. But surely, you're not going instead of your sister?

Won't Mr Osgood be expecting a woman?"

"Lucy's in Nottingham with our aunt. I won't have an opportunity to discuss a plan until her return tomorrow. My idea at the moment, if she should agree, is for me to hide as soon as it's dark and for her to meet Osgood as arranged in the lychgate and for me to rush him. I'm hoping he doesn't know I'm here in Linderbourne and he'll believe Lucy is alone and defenceless. When she hands over the money, it'll give me a chance to creep up on them and take it back. I'll threaten to ensure my uncle dismisses him without references if he should tell anyone what he saw and if that fails I shall punch him on the nose." He laughed.

"Mr Gregory! This is no laughing matter! John Osgood is a prize-fighter. He's not afraid to use his knuckles."

"Do I detect a slight amount of concern?" he asked, his thumb gently stroking the back of her hand.

She swallowed. Her mouth had gone dry. "I... I wouldn't want to see you get hurt."

"You don't appear to have much confidence in me!"

"John Osgood is a bully. He is at home using his fists. I know this and so does my brother, Henry."

His hand tightened over hers.

"In that case, I'll definitely punch him as well as threatening him with dismissal."

"Please take this seriously. He's not a fool." Her stomach lurched. Mr Gregory couldn't possibly realise what sort of brute he'd be dealing with. How could she make him understand?

"Then I shall take note of the numbers on the banknotes and accuse him of robbery. When the constable searches his cottage, he'll find the money."

"But how will you explain being out at night with money whose numbers you'd thought to record? Does that not look suspicious?"

"I didn't say my plan was perfect," he said, "it has certain flaws."

"Now I know you're not taking this seriously."

"You're right. But I assure you, I've been thinking of little else since I learnt of the letter. However, until Lucy returns, I can't make a decision."

"Is your sister brave enough to agree to meet him in such a quiet place in the dark?"

"I truly don't know. She has courage and will be keen to rescue her reputation."

Keziah shuddered at the thought of encountering John Osgood on her own in the dark and wondered whether the girl would understand how much danger she was in.

"Come!" he said, "I'm delaying you and the evening breeze is cool." He removed his top hand from hers and for a second, she thought he would lift hers to his lips but after a moment's hesitation, he let it go.

"I wish you goodnight, Miss Bonner." He smiled at her and then, leading the horse, he turned the gig around to face the other way with great difficulty as the road was narrow.

He didn't look back but she raised her hand to wave goodbye anyway and the evening breeze wafted the scent of sandalwood which had transferred to her skin from his. She buried her face in her palm as she made her way into the building.

...Seven, eight, nine.

Mathew waited for the next chime but the clock in the valley was silent.

Surely it was later than nine o'clock? Perhaps he'd woken after the chimes had begun and he'd counted incorrectly?

He sat up and looked at the clock on the mantelshelf. Two things struck him: first, that it was indeed nine o'clock in the morning and second, his head wasn't thumping.

He reached out and tugged on the bell-pull by his bed for Jefferson. Unusually, he felt rested and alert and was keen to start the day, and that was just as well, as he needed to spend as much time as he could with Lucy planning the following night's meeting with the blackmailer.

He'd kept the conversation with Keziah light the previous evening, trying to conceal his anxiety. Not that he was worried for himself – he knew how to fight with his fists, a sword or a pistol. But if Osgood – if it was indeed him – were to start a rumour about Lucy... It might not just ruin her reputation and her chance of a good marriage, it might push Uncle Obadiah to his limits.

Matthew had sorely tried Uncle Obadiah with his enormous debts. Now, if it was discovered that Lucy had been consorting with a carpenter in the woods and had disgraced the Rigbys, their uncle might decide to cut all ties with his wife's family.

Obadiah Rigby was a generous, upright man. True, he was rather puritanical and very careful with his money, which is probably how he'd built up such a successful business and managed to amass a huge fortune. He was moderate in everything he did – neither drinking nor eating to excess – and definitely not indulging in the other vices that were enjoyed by the gentility who so snobbishly rejected him.

Had anyone known he'd been supporting his brother-in-law's family for many years, they may well have wondered why. Matthew was aware his father was not fond of Obadiah, but then, Father was a sick man and after Robert had died, he no longer seemed to have a liking for anyone, especially his second son. Matthew had believed Uncle Obadiah's continuing support for his brother-in-law was explained by his strong sense of duty… That is, until his friend, Felix Sparham, had told him about an event that had taken place many years before.

Aunt Hannah had fallen in love with Obadiah Rigby but Sir Hugh had been appalled and had refused to give his permission for the couple to marry. The young Obadiah's fortune might well have compensated for his lack of breeding in Sir Hugh's eyes but the fact that he worked for a living, meant he was absolutely inappropriate as a prospective husband for the sister of a baronet. Sir Hugh was adamant she would not be allowed to humiliate the family – that is, until someone insulted Hannah and her would-be suitor, within his hearing. Then, there had been no alternative. Sir Hugh had challenged the man to a duel and Felix's father, had agreed to be his second.

With his first shot, Sir Hugh missed his opponent but he was struck in the shoulder. It had been a flesh wound and by the time it had been dressed, Sir Hugh had lost a large amount of blood. That night, he'd suffered an apoplectic fit and from that day on, his health had deteriorated.

Previously, Matthew had considered the strained relationship between his father and the Rigbys was regrettable and under the circumstances, his uncle's generosity towards Father was remarkable. But Felix's revelation had made everything clear. Uncle Obadiah felt guilty and ashamed that his wife's brother had suffered so much because of him.

But how long would that obligation persist? Would he one day consider he'd paid his debt in full? Certainly, if Uncle Obadiah gained a place in society, he might consider he no longer needed to feel guilty or ashamed. Already he'd won a certain amount of acceptance by funding the nearby town's new assembly rooms and he'd just taken up his place as a magistrate. It was possible that he and Aunt Hannah might one day be fully accepted into local society. It might be different in London, but his aunt and uncle seemed happy living in Linderbourne.

A shock such as Lucy's outrageous behaviour might well force Uncle Obadiah to cut all ties with his sister's family; first, to save money and then, to distance itself from the scandal that Lucy's behaviour would inevitably bring.

When Jefferson arrived, Matthew asked when the family would be returning, only to discover they'd been invited to a ball on Saturday evening and would not return until late on Sunday.

Poor Lucy! She'd be so worried. He hoped she wouldn't do anything rash like ride back unaccompanied. That would merely raise questions she wouldn't want to answer.

So, it was up to him to save the family and his sister's reputation.

Keziah had woken weary and swollen-eyed on Saturday morning. She'd barely slept for worrying that Mr Gregory appeared to have very little idea about what to expect when he and his sister confronted Osgood later that evening. The plan to meet the blackmailer and to threaten him was sheer folly. But she couldn't think of a better scheme. Everything had to be done without giving away Miss Gregory's secret. That meant the fewer people who were involved the better. Osgood had to be stopped.

Mr Gregory was completely unprepared. And what would happen if he couldn't overcome Osgood? He'd said he knew how to fight with his fists but she doubted he'd ever fought anyone like the burly overlooker. And what might become of Miss Gregory? If Osgood gained the upper hand, he could act with impunity, knowing he had Mr Rigby's nephew and niece in his power.

Even worse, when Keziah arrived at work, it became clear Osgood was in a foul mood after his accident the previous day. He'd brought a cudgel to work with him and had leaned it against the wall by the door. Although he hadn't used it, he was even more brutal than usual, lashing out at the apprentices with hands and feet, especially Henry who received several blows.

Had he brought the cudgel ready for meeting Miss Gregory later? Keziah wished she could get word to Mr Gregory to warn him he should come armed but she doubted she was even going to be allowed out early to get to the schoolhouse on time for lessons.

However, as Keziah nervously approached Osgood for permission to leave, one of the youngest girls screamed and fainted. As she was being hauled from beneath the machinery where she'd been reaching for some waste cotton, Osgood unlocked the door to call for the mill surgeon and he waved Keziah away. She wasn't sure he'd really meant her to leave but if she'd stayed, he would undoubtedly have kept her back, so she slipped out, her heart racing twice as fast as her feet as she ran down the stairs and out of the mill.

Now what? She could hardly appear at Linderbourne Hall and ask for Mr Matthew Gregory. That would put him in a very difficult situation if his uncle saw her.

She'd spent the entire walk from the Apprentice House to the schoolhouse pondering how to warn him and his sister about Osgood's foul mood and, more importantly, the cudgel, but other than trying to intercept them before they arrived later that night, any steps she took to contact them, might result in others finding out. She glanced across the road to the church and the lychgate, where, in a few hours, Miss Gregory would meet Osgood. A flash of blue caught her eye. Someone wearing a blue cloak had entered the church and closed the door. It was a colour unlikely to be worn by any man who lived in this valley and the women, who would have been most happy to own such a garment, couldn't have afforded it... all except a member of the Rigby household.

It was either Mrs Rigby or her niece, Miss Gregory. Or perhaps both. Keziah decided to find out and walked across the road towards the church and quietly entered. At first, the cold interior of the church appeared to be empty and she wondered if she'd been mistaken, then she saw a figure sitting in the corner of the Lady Chapel, kneeling in an attitude of prayer with her hood pulled down.

Perhaps Lucy Gregory had come to ask for forgiveness? Keziah didn't like to disturb someone at prayer but it was important she warned the girl – for her own safety and for that of her brother. Yet, she hesitated. Perhaps she'd be finished soon and there would be no need to interrupt. But time was passing and she needed to get back to the school before the children arrived, so she softly cleared her throat and deliberately allowed her skirt to swish.

The blue-clad figure remained kneeling.

Keziah wondered what to do and then, she caught sight of the bottom of the boots that were not quite covered by the azure cloak.

"Mr Gregory!" she whispered before she could stop herself. Immediately, the figure turned and she saw it was indeed him. His face was flushed but he looked relieved when he recognised her.

"This probably requires an explanation..." he said with a rueful smile, throwing back the hood.

# CHAPTER SIX

"You look nothing like a lady." Keziah shook her head in dismay and watched him walk up the aisle once again.

In response, he stood on tiptoe and attempted to move in the way he imagined a woman might daintily advance. If it hadn't been so serious, Keziah would have laughed.

"Osgood is no fool, he'll be on his guard and if the weather clears, the full moon will make it easy to see you're not a girl. And even if he doesn't notice, and you take him by surprise, you won't be able to defend yourself encumbered with a cloak."

"Without Lucy, that's the best I can do."

"There is another option." She stifled a giggle as he tried to mince down the aisle again. "Once school has finished, I'll come back. In that cloak, I'll play the part of your sister and then, you..." she hadn't added anything else as she wasn't sure what he'd do to Osgood.

Mr Gregory refused at first but the good sense of her plan was unquestionable – if indeed, there was such a thing as a good plan to deal with this situation.

"Even so, that's no reason to endanger you," he said.

"I believe there'll be less danger if we work together. I'm keen to see Osgood dismissed. It'll make life easier for Henry and me."

"Ah!" he said, his voice teasing, "so, you're doing this for purely selfish reasons?"

"No! Yes, no..." The words tripped over themselves making her feel thoroughly foolish. To reply that she was acting solely for herself wasn't true and it seemed cold and unfeeling. Yet, to admit to wanting to help him, suggested she cared about him and that simply wasn't true. And if it had been true, she certainly wouldn't have wanted him to know. She could imagine how, one day in the future when he'd returned to London, he'd laugh at the young would-be schoolmistress who'd been so smitten with him she'd agreed to stand in for his sister and risk... well, who knew what she was risking? But the thought of him ridiculing her to Lord This and Sir That filled her with anger.

"Actually," she said, "I'm doing this so that I'll have no reason to see you ever again... That is, I mean..." She cringed. Surely it would have been better to have claimed to be doing it for selfish reasons than to have tried to be so hurtful for something of which he hadn't actually been guilty.

"Yes, yes of course," he said in a formal voice, "and please know I'm very grateful, as will Lucy be, if we can make this scheme work. I understand your wish to be rid of me. I will respect that. However, since I'll be living in the area, I can't guarantee you won't see me out and about. But please be assured I won't trouble you again."

"Are you not going back to London?" she asked, her surprise overcoming her embarrassment at her rudeness.

He looked up towards the wooden beams of the roof and bit the bottom corner of his lip. "No... I will not be going back to London." His voice was flat and emotionless but he didn't offer an explanation.

Indeed, why should he? She had the impression his decision – if indeed it was his decision – not to return to London did not please him.

"There are certain obligations I must meet before I can return to London," he said and then he'd taken the cloak off with a sigh.

After school finished, Keziah took her time tidying away, then ensured no one saw her as she crossed the road and entered the church. The road was wet and the leaves in the hedges weighed down with raindrops from the heavy shower that had fallen shortly before school had ended. It must have lasted long enough to chase anyone indoors who might otherwise have been abroad – other than one man who staggered out of the alehouse and wove his way back and forth across the road heading away from the church. But she saw no one else. John Osgood's cottage, she knew, was at the far end of the village and he would not be able to observe her from there.

She opened the church door as quietly as she could. "Mr Gregory!" she whispered into the stone-cold, echoing blackness. She wondered if perhaps he'd become bored with waiting and had returned to the Hall.

"I'm here," he said from behind the door, making her jump, "But since we're partners in this plan, you might do me the honour of using my given name. If you need help, calling 'Matthew' will be faster than 'Mr Gregory'. And perhaps, I may call you 'Keziah'?"

"So long as you remember I'm 'Lucy' while Osgood is in earshot!"

Matthew was silent for a few moments, "I don't like this at all," he said finally, keeping his voice low, "you have so much to lose if things go wrong and he discovers your identity."

"I believe I can do it," Keziah whispered.

"I can see you are determined. The question is, how will I forgive myself if anything happens to you?"

He drew her into the church and closed the door. "Come, follow me," he said and keeping his hand on her arm, he whispered, "let us sit awhile and talk. It it hadn't been for the thought the curate might come in and want to know why I was sitting in his church on my own, I do believe I would have nodded off with boredom." "Have you been here the entire time I've been in school?"

"Yes, I spent some time inspecting the graveyard. I didn't want to stumble in the darkness and I could hardly have come later with a lantern and announced myself. But now, tell me what you've been doing." Still holding her arm, he reached out with the other hand and guided them to a nearby pew where they sat in the icy, echoing silence of the church and she told him about her evening. It was disconcerting to be so close to him in the darkness. Periodically, the moon shone through a gap in the clouds and pearly light penetrated the lofty, arched windows, allowing her to see his face. She didn't need to see him to know how close he was to her. She could feel his warmth and his breath on her cheek. But that was a sensible precaution because the closer they were, the easier it was for him to hear her whispers and the less likelihood there was of anyone finding them.

"You're cold," she said, jumping as his hand brushed hers.

"Frozen to the bone. In fact, I'm not sure I can feel my fingers any longer."

She held his hand between hers and tried to warm him. Her palms moulded around his long, slender fingers and she remembered watching him move the letter the first time they'd met – was it only a few days ago? And how he'd placed them over hers on the broom handle. How beautiful they were, how sensitive and the memory of him stroking her hands made her grow warmer.

She hadn't had such prolonged contact with another person since before she and Henry had been taken into the workhouse. That life seemed so far away and she hadn't wanted to talk about it, nor to think about it and especially not to cast her mind back to her childhood. That had stopped the day she'd entered the workhouse. But he'd asked her about her life before she'd come to Linderbourne and once she'd started to tell him, it had been painful – as she'd expected – but also a relief to share everything.

She told him about her father's successful watchmakers' shop in Black Swan Lane, in the middle of Westminster and how first Mama had died, shortly after giving birth to Henry then five years later, Papa had followed her into St Margaret's graveyard. While the Bonner children, fourteen-year-old Eva; Keziah, aged ten and Henry, aged five, were at his funeral, the shop was stripped of clocks, watches, tools and anything else of value by Papa's partner, who also emptied the bank account, leaving nothing for the Bonner orphans.

Strange, she thought, the only person with whom she'd shared her past, was someone who she'd have formerly considered a selfish, spoilt man with no capacity to feel for anyone else, especially someone from an inferior class. Yet, although she was unable to see his expression, she could feel his compassion, and no longer was his hand sandwiched between hers. Somehow, during her account, he'd taken both of hers and was holding them protectively.

"And then you went to the workhouse?" he prompted her.

She hesitated. What happened next had haunted her nightmares for years but it was too raw to share. How could she tell him they'd been tricked by a high-class bawd, and that Keziah had been so furious with Eva, she'd set things in motion that would see her sister convicted of a crime she hadn't committed and being transported halfway across the world to the penal colony in New South Wales? What would he think of her?

"Yes, we went to the workhouse." And then to return to the truth, she added. "I was such a stubborn child. I thought I knew it all..."

"I envy you your confidence and certainty. At least you did what you thought was right. I, on the other hand, have always done what's easy. When I was very young, I tried my best but I never matched up to my elder brother, Robert. He had the advantage of four years, so I could never have equalled him when we were boys but later, as men, my father always celebrated his successes. He never saw mine. In the end, I gave up. What's the point in always failing? It's better not to try. At least in that, I'm a success. My father can't forgive me for living while his favourite son died, so he looks at me and he sees a failure and I constantly live up to his expectations."

"Oh, Matthew, I'm so sorry. How easy it is to assume anyone with money is living an enjoyable life." Even though he'd requested she use his given name, it had felt so strange on her lips because she knew it was not appropriate behaviour. But sitting hand in hand in the dark had removed all the usual barriers as if no one else existed.

"As for money," he said bitterly, "I don't have any. I have to rely on my uncle's generosity. All my fault, of course. I spend too long at the card tables. It's the only time I feel alive – just before the card is turned – the excitement is breath-taking. And the greater the stakes, the more thrilling it is. But lately, my losses have been huge. And I have yet to share that bit of bad news with my uncle and to beg him to help me once more."

"Is that why you can't go back to London?"

"I could go back. I'm simply not sure I want to. If Uncle pays my debts as he usually does, I could go back to my old life as if nothing had changed. Father would complain about me, so I'd go to my club, to the theatre, to places I'd rather not tell you about and... well anywhere, looking for somewhere to belong. And then when my allowance had gone, I'd be back, begging Uncle Obadiah to bail me out. But since I've been here and more specifically, since I met you, and have glimpsed into your life, I've seen another way."

"How could my life possibly have shown you anything?"

He paused and leaned his forehead against hers, "It's not your life, it's how you lead it. You've experienced so much and yet you have aspirations. I have so much but I look no further than the next ball or social gathering."

With his head against hers, Keziah could barely breathe.

He continued, "I thought I knew all about the world but in fact, I know very little. It's like I've been shut up in a room all my life and have suddenly been let outside into the real world. There was so much going on around me I didn't notice. But now, I can see possibilities and chances to succeed. Of course, ever since I met you, I've done nothing but fail – I know I've caused you many problems and I'm truly sorry. But that's enough about me. I want to hear more of your life..."

A few minutes before ten o'clock, Keziah was on the road leading from Linderbourne Hall into the village. Wearing the blue cloak with the hood pulled forward to conceal her face, she was half-hidden in the hedgerow, waiting for the first chime of the church clock – her signal to step out onto the road as if she'd just arrived on foot from the Hall. Matthew was hidden somewhere in the churchyard although she had no idea where and could only hope he was close enough to assist her, should she need his help.

As the clapper hit the bell, she crept out of her hiding place and forced herself to stride purposefully towards the crossroads where she turned left towards the lychgate. Ominous, grey clouds raced across the face of the full moon, threatening more heavy rain and deepening the night. Keziah peered into the gloom for a sign of anyone. But Osgood, if he was already there, wasn't visible. Not surprising, since he'd chosen the meeting place wisely with its dark shadows into which a man could vanish.

A cold wind plucked at the edges of the cloak and she snatched at them, pulling the blue velvet over the skirt which, if seen up close, might give her away as a girl who didn't belong to the gentry. With the thought of the ruthless overlooker waiting in the shadows, and his fury, should he discover her identity, her pace slackened. She told herself to take daintier steps to look more like a lady and less like a harassed apprentice girl, not wanting to admit it also slowed her progress towards the encounter she was dreading.

She could see no one. Could Osgood see her?

Could Matthew?

Why couldn't she hear something?

Anything?

Keziah stopped a few yards short of the lychgate, straining to detect the slightest sound above the pounding of her heart and her own ragged breaths. But the sturdy, ivy-covered roof, cast a shadow so deep that anyone standing beneath the lychgate, would simply appear to be black on black.

*Breathe,* she told herself, as she became aware her vision was beginning to swim and a strange feeling of disconnectedness washed over her.

She must not faint now.

She would not allow it.

At the scuff of a boot against the ground a yard or so in front of her, Keziah stumbled backwards with a gasp. A shadowy figure, clad in a black cloak with a hood pulled forward, detached itself from the darkness. He silently extended his arm as if telling her to place the money on his outstretched hand. With the man's back to the lychgate, Keziah knew it would be impossible for Matthew to take him by surprise. She needed to lure him out. Yet, she couldn't bear the thought of him drawing any closer to her.

Where was Matthew?

The hooded stranger's fingers beckoned impatiently and from the depths of the hood, a gruff voice said, "Hand it over!"

Keziah nearly dropped the packet Matthew had given her containing the money, in shock. It didn't sound like John Osgood. Too deep, too rasping.

Hold your nerve! Of course, he would try to disguise his voice. Like her, he had his hood pulled forward concealing his face and was obviously taking great pains not to be identified.

Where was Matthew? There was not a whisper nor a flicker of movement.

The cloaked figure took a half-step towards her and at that instant, a gap in the clouds allowed the full moon to shine brightly on the scene, illuminating the churchyard with shocking clarity. But still, there was no sign of Matthew. Startled at the silvery light, the man paused and lowered his head, pulling his hood further forward with stubby fingers that she recognised. Yes, despite the disguised voice and the hooded cloak, she knew the man whose hand was outstretched, demanding money was definitely John Osgood.

Well, at least she knew who they were dealing with but she had to stall for time to give Matthew the chance to get Osgood before he walked away with the money and was gone. It was possible, he had a horse ready to leave that night, in which case, it was unlikely he'd ever be caught and he'd escape with Matthew's money.

How could she distract him without speaking and giving away her identity?

She could surely say one or two words in an upper class accent but much more than that and he might guess she was an imposter. She turned the packet over in her hands and then had the idea of dropping it. The clouds were once again obscuring the moon and taking advantage of the cover of darkness, she gave what she hoped was an upper class squeal of alarm as she allowed it to slip from her grasp. She crouched to retrieve it and as she fumbled for the package, she managed to push it further away from him.

Keziah retrieved it and stood as Osgood stepped out of the shadows with an annoyed grunt. He extended his hand to snatch it from her but over his shoulder, Keziah glimpsed a rapid movement as Matthew leapt from the churchyard wall and landing lightly behind Osgood, he threw his arm around the cloaked figure's neck, jerking his head backwards. With a swift tug, Matthew pulled the hood back, exposing the man's face. In response, Osgood reached inside his cloak and brought out a cudgel. Matthew was too quick for him, grabbing his wrist and wrenching his arm backwards until he dropped the weapon. It rolled towards Keziah who picked it up. Her instinct was to hurl it as far as she could to prevent any violence from taking place but if, God forbid, Osgood should overpower Matthew, she might need to defend herself.

"Please, no!" she whispered over and over at the thought of swinging the club and even worse, the prospect of making contact.

But Matthew was still in control. Osgood's hands clawed at Matthew's arm, trying to prise it off his neck but he was off-balance, being dragged backwards.

"Well, Osgood, what do you think your employer would say about this if he were to find out?" Matthew whispered. He was out of breath with the effort of holding the larger, stockier man.

"Let me go!" Osgood gasped, then turning his face towards Keziah, he said, "I told you not to tell anyone! Too bad, your secret will soon be out."

Matthew tightened the grip around his throat cutting off Osgood's threat.

"I don't think so," Matthew said, "If my sister's secret gets out, I shall make it my business to ensure my uncle is informed about where the rumour started and how you attempted blackmail. Then, it will be your word against my sister's. I will back my sister up in any way I can to save her reputation. Yet, you will be seen as a would-be blackmailer. I would exert the utmost pressure on my uncle, who holds my opinion in great esteem, for soon I'll be his business partner. It will be your word against mine... And I wouldn't lay odds on your chances. So, my advice to you would be to remain silent and keep your job and home. What do you say?"

Matthew released his grip and with a great push, thrust Osgood away. The overlooker fell to his knees and took in gulps of air, his hands to his throat. When he'd caught his breath, he lumbered to his feet and stood some way from Matthew. "You're forgetting," he said, his voice hoarse, "it won't be your word against mine, it'll be your word against mine and my brother's!" He laughed, "You can't have forgotten about Tom. Remember he was there, he can give details..."

And with that, Osgood turned and called over his shoulder, "You'll be hearing from me again. Don't think this is the end of the matter." Then he staggered away, into the village.

Matthew and Keziah stood silently for a few seconds watching until the night swallowed him up.

"Now what do we do?" Keziah asked, "he's right, Tom will back him up. Who would dare refuse that monster anything?"

"I had hoped a little intimidation would put an end to it," Matthew admitted with a sigh. "Apparently not, but at least we've delayed things. Now he knows he won't simply be able to take money from Lucy whenever he feels like it. Although whether that will drive him to increase his demand so he has enough to make it worth running away from Linderbourne, I have no idea. The only way this could truly have been resolved would have been if Osgood had met with an unfortunate accident. Then Lucy would be safe." His voice was harsh with bitterness.

"Matthew! Surely you're not suggesting you should have caused such an accident?" His frustration was understandable, but surely, he hadn't considered harming Osgood? She suddenly realised she was holding the cudgel and with distaste, she dropped it to the ground.

Matthew bent to pick it up in silence. Finally, without answering her question, he said, "Once again, I'm in your debt and must beg your pardon for keeping you so late and thank you for all you've done for Lucy and me. Let's dispose of this." He held up Osgood's club, "and then I'll escort you home."

She handed him the envelope. "At least you saved the money."

He laughed. "That envelope is stuffed with paper. There's nothing of value in there. I barely have five guineas, let alone fifty. Come..." He led her to the bridge over the river and dropped the cudgel into the dark water below.

Keziah unfastened the clasp of the cloak and began to swing it from her shoulders.

"No, don't take it off. It's cold, leave it on until you get home. I think you should keep it. I'm sure Lucy would agree."

"Thank you. That's most kind but such a beautiful garment would be noticed and I'd probably be accused of stealing it because everyone would know I couldn't afford something so wonderful."

He sighed. "Yes, I can see you have a point... But at least keep it on until you get home. The wind's cold tonight."

"Here, let me help you," he said as she tried to fasten the clasp again.

He placed his hands over hers and once the cloak was secure, he kept hold of her hands and raised them both to his lips.

"No!" She drew away from him. "Please don't!"

"Why ever not? We've both just stared death in the face." He smiled at her but didn't let go of her hands.

"Hardly!" she said laughing.

"Yes!" he insisted, "And there's nothing like a shared near-death experience, to forge a bond between two people."

Of course, he was joking with her but there was indeed, a special excitement borne of having conspired and – if they hadn't exactly won – well, they hadn't lost either. They'd worked together, as equals.

Matthew let go of one hand but continued to hold the other and she didn't attempt to pull it from him.

It was warm. It was comforting. And on this strange, dark night, where she was filled with the thrill of having overcome her terror, it felt perfect.

The unusual atmosphere seemed to have affected Matthew in the same way because he said, "When I was a young boy, I used to imagine there was a secret door and if you went through, you'd find yourself in what I called, the Other Place. It was somewhere you could forget who you were and what people expected you to be. There would be no recriminations and no consequences, just the memories to carry with you when you came back through the door into real life."

"That sounds very appealing. For so long, I've been trying to control real life with no great success. I haven't had much time to dream – well, not unless you count my hopes of being a schoolmistress one day. I've never thought of trying to be someone else but it would be lovely to leave behind all responsibility and to try out something new."

"Then let's go there!"

"To your Other Place?" She stopped and looked at him in confusion.

"Yes!" he said breathlessly, his eyes shining with excitement.

"How? There's no such thing as a secret door..."

"Then, let's imagine we're already through it. We have from here to the Apprentice House, to be who we want to be. There's no one else around to see or to judge. We could just be Matthew and Keziah – no history, no worries about the future – just the present and our dreams. What do you think?"

"I...I..." This was madness. But she so wanted to share it.

"Come on! What is there to lose?" He stopped abruptly and taking both her hands, he said, "I wouldn't hurt you, Keziah, you know that, don't you? I don't want to take advantage of you, I just want to forget the difference in our class and to meet as equals. I think after tonight, we deserve that, don't we?"

How enticing it was to believe in the Other Place where their relative positions in life meant nothing, even if only for the time it took to walk to the Apprentice House.

"Yes," she whispered.

For once, the woods that loomed on either side of the road didn't offer a threat – they added to the enchantment of the private world they'd created, as they talked about everything and nothing, about make-believe and dreams, but avoiding anything that threatened to drag them back into reality. Gradually, at first, without even realising it, their steps became slower and slower to prolong their time together but finally, when they arrived at the last bend in the road before the forbidding, grey building, they stopped for fear of being spotted from one of the windows. It was highly unlikely anyone would still be awake, much less peering out, but there was no need to take unnecessary risks.

Keziah fumbled with the clasp to the cloak but before she could undo it, Matthew had grasped either side of the hood and gently pulled her face towards him, brushing her lips with his. He immediately released her and stepped back. Was he trying to judge her reaction or perhaps showing her he wasn't a threat? He looked so young and boyish, his usual sophistication gone, as if in this world they'd created, he really had become someone different.

Forgetting the clasp, she touched two fingers to her mouth. Had their lips met? Her common sense told her their faces had touched in the dark. Merely an accident. But her lips told her otherwise. They tingled with the memory and when she ran her tongue over them, she fancied she could taste him.

Nonsense!

But for once, she ignored her common sense. After all, in this make-believe place they'd created, she could be anyone and act out any part she chose. Neither of them would ever refer to this time again. She would have no reason to spend time with Matthew in the future, indeed, if she ever met him again, she would address him as Mr Gregory and other than to glimpse him occasionally perhaps on horseback in the village or at the mill with his uncle, they would never be alone like this.

Still, he watched her, and she knew he was waiting to see her reaction. But, how, she wondered, did she let him know she longed for their lips to touch again. Not simply to skim across each other lightly in something that had almost been a kiss, but to press against each other, to... to... she realised she had no idea what might happen next but the possibility of anything happening at all, filled her with a warmth that welled up from deep inside and she gasped involuntarily, as it took her breath away.

Matthew took another step backwards. "I'm sorry!" he said in alarm, mistaking her reaction. "Please forgive me!"

She didn't have the words to explain, and if she had, she doubted she could have said them. But she didn't want him to leave thinking he'd upset her. In fact, she didn't want him to leave at all. Not before they'd really kissed.

This was a now or never moment that could only happen in the Other Place.

Keziah moved towards him and hesitantly placed her palms on his chest. It had been a preliminary step towards linking her hands behind his neck, so she hadn't expected to feel his muscles tense beneath the linen of his shirt. Neither had she anticipated the heady hints of sandalwood mingled with his masculine scent would fill her nostrils. For the second time that evening, she had to remind herself to breathe as her mind seemed to float. But this wasn't fear such as she'd felt earlier, this was something that consumed her. Something that coursed through her body like a rushing torrent.

The horrified expression on his face had been replaced by wonder and then eagerness as she gently slid her hands over the smooth shirt to rest lightly on the back of his neck. He cupped her face with his hands and gently caressed her cheeks with his thumbs. Then, leaning towards her

– as she'd longed for him to do – he hesitated for an instant before placing his lips over hers.

With Matthew's kiss still singing on her lips, Keziah crept up the stairs to the dormitory and discovered that for once, Becky had returned before her. She quietly climbed into the cot, still aware of the pressure of his hands on her shoulders, at the back of her head and the caress of his breath on her cheek. She'd given herself up to the strange feelings that had possessed her while she'd been in Matthew's arms. Too soon, he'd unlaced her fingers and taken her hands from his neck, then after planting a kiss on each palm, he bade her goodnight and turned to go. She'd been so disappointed, she'd almost forgotten to give him the blue, velvet cloak and after helping her with the clasp, he'd taken it and walked quickly away, looking back once to blow her a kiss.

Keziah curled up next to Becky, remembering the walk from the bridge to the Apprentice House. But most of all, she relived her first kiss. Over and over again.

She and Matthew had stepped outside of time. It would never happen again. There would never be any circumstances that would lead them to that Other Place on any other occasion. So, she committed every single detail to her memory.

On his walk back to Linderbourne Hall, Matthew's mind was whirling. Nothing had been resolved, he'd simply delayed matters. Would he have dealt with Osgood differently, if Keziah had not been there? He'd taken the precaution of carrying a dagger with him but although that would have solved one problem, it would have thrown up many more. And anyway, he suspected Keziah would have been vehemently against the use of his knife even though she and her brother were often the bully's victims.

Keziah.

She filled his mind. For Lucy's sake, he tried to push all thoughts of her away and focus on the question of Osgood. At least everyone's position was now clear. Osgood knew Lucy had an ally and Matthew knew Osgood was still prepared to demand money and would use his brother to corroborate his story. Who was in the stronger position? Matthew hated to admit it but it seemed the overlooker had the upper hand. He ran the last few seconds of the encounter through his mind again.

"You'll be hearing from me again. Don't think this is the end of the matter."

Once again, Keziah's face appeared in his imagination. How courageous she'd been and how clever to have dropped the package she believed contained banknotes to keep it from Osgood and to lure him into the open. He could feel her palms pressed against his chest. His heart beating wildly at her touch. And those lips...

Keziah.

Stop! You must concentrate on solving the problem. This could still be a disaster for Lucy.

He dragged his mind back to Osgood.

Despite having told the overlooker otherwise, Matthew recognised that if rumours were started, he wouldn't be able to let his uncle know where they'd begun. Uncle Obadiah would surely ask Matthew what evidence he had to link them to Osgood and, worse, his knowledge of such a story would probably even confirm its truth. His uncle would undoubtedly question the overlooker and when he also heard Tom Osgood's side of the story, he'd have no choice but to believe it was true. What would happen then? Certainly, Lucy's life would be ruined. It would put Uncle Obadiah in a difficult position too.

If only Lucy wasn't so impetuous! Matthew had once admired what he'd considered was her bravery, but compared to Keziah, he realised she simply rushed headlong into situations with no thought for the outcome. That wasn't bravery, it was sheer recklessness. Earlier that evening, he'd trusted Keziah and she hadn't let him down. Had Lucy been there, he mused, she might have stood her ground or she might not. She'd have been unpredictable, and as much as he loved her, he suspected she'd have acted thoughtlessly and impulsively, possibly even endangering herself and him.

He sighed. He and Lucy were so alike.

Or were they?

He most definitely had been thoughtless and impulsive. He'd raised those qualities to an art form. But now? Something had changed in his reasoning. He'd changed.

Inconsiderate, shallow, heedless. Lacking capacity for thought. All criticisms levelled at him by his father. But were they still true? Could someone change so completely?

He'd cared deeply about what happened to Keziah, that evening. So much so, he'd waited longer than he'd intended before pouncing to ensure she was far enough away from Osgood that she wouldn't be hurt. He'd identified something admirable in Keziah that he knew his sister lacked.

A thoughtless man would surely not have noticed. And a person who weighed situations up and cared about the outcome could no longer be considered thoughtless. Could they?

He wasn't sure. Thoughtlessness wasn't a concept he'd have considered a few weeks ago. It had certainly been easier to think and make decisions since he'd been at Linderbourne Hall. His mind was clearer and he wondered whether it was the country air or more likely, because he no longer drank to excess. Each morning, he felt more alive than the day before and realised with a shock it was because he didn't wake each day with a headache after drinking himself to a stupor the previous evening. The oppressive malaise and numbness had occurred each morning with such regularity, he'd begun to believe it was normal. To begin with, he'd drunk to forget his inadequacy. It was something of which his father had often reminded him but somehow, the alcohol blunted the criticism.

It had also changed his perception of danger. His friend, Felix, had a wild streak, taking part in the most outrageous wagers. He'd survived a knockout during a boxing match with a prize-fighter, escaped unscathed after being thrown from a horse one moonless night as he'd ridden five miles at breakneck speed to break the previous record. And, he'd recovered from a ducking in a frozen lake when the ice cracked, sending him plunging beneath. He had no regard for his safety – nor anyone else's and Matthew had often taken part in those mad escapades with him. Being younger and fitter, Matthew had so far not been hurt and had thoroughly enjoyed the thrill of the danger. Each time he conquered his fear, he felt he'd proved something to his father. Then later, recognising Father neither knew nor cared what he'd done, he'd drunk himself to oblivion.

But now, it was as if he was outside his body, observing and judging himself. And he didn't like what he saw.

If he could solve the Osgood problem, he'd take Lucy to one side and try to make her understand they must both change. Not only because Uncle Obadiah would lose patience with them but because they both needed to come to their senses.

The main difficulty was going to be Tom Osgood. After all, he'd been there with Lucy and as his brother had pointed out, he would be able to give details. But if Tom Osgood disappeared...

Yes! That was the answer.

Matthew had the perfect solution. Felix owed him a large sum of money. He was also building a house in London – the main reason why he was temporarily unable to pay Matthew. If Felix were to offer Tom Osgood a job as a carpenter working on his house, he wouldn't be there to confirm his brother's story. And it would allow him to escape from his bullying brother too.

Having come up with a solution for Lucy, Matthew's mind turned once again to Keziah. She intrigued him. He'd had many girls. Some had thrown themselves at him and others had been wilier; enticing him with the thrill of the chase but there'd always been an ulterior motive, from attempting to ensnare him into marriage or more simply indulging in a night of pleasure. However, the young mill girl, with her courage and spark didn't strike him as someone who'd lead him on for her own ends. Hadn't she repeatedly told him to leave her alone? No one had ever filled his mind as Keziah had done since the evening he'd tried to intimidate her in the schoolhouse. How magnificent she was, despite her lack of silks and satins. And how fragile...

She was the only person with whom he'd ever shared the Other Place – he'd never even told Lucy. It had been his escape into a world where he could be the son his father wanted or indeed, he could be anyone he chose. Keziah had understood. She'd played along with him. But he'd had enough sense to realise it wouldn't take much to frighten her. She was attracted to him, he knew, but she'd told him enough about her life before Linderbourne for him to know she was determined to lift herself up and to become independent. Nothing would stand in the way of that and she would not be a girl to play with.

And yet, she'd responded to his touch; he'd felt her quiver with anticipation, as delicate and as skittish as a butterfly. Hardly surprising for someone who had been repeatedly knocked down that she should be wary of anything new. And he was sure this was something new for her. At first, she'd been tremulous but she'd quickly learnt how to respond and her eagerness had touched something deep inside him. The many women he'd known were like shadows with no substance or meaning. But Keziah. He could still taste her, feel her body pressed against him and his heart beating in time with hers.

Matthew awoke early. For so many years, he slept late and missed this time of golden light. Of course, he'd often arrived home at first light and then slept most of the day but waking up to the dawn was something new.

His thoughts immediately turned to Keziah and he hoped she'd slept well after such a strange night. He knew her day would not be as hectic as usual because it was Sunday and she would be required to go to church and to lead Sunday School unless Miss Maynard had returned to work.

He wondered what would happen to Keziah once the schoolmistress was well enough to carry out her duties.

That brief time before the apprentices arrived at the school and after they'd gone, were the times when he knew he'd be able to see Keziah – should he need to – but that would finish once Miss Maynard was back.

Since Lucy would be home later that day, he reminded himself he wouldn't need to see Keziah again and that thought drew at his insides as if he'd lost something precious.

What was the matter with him? She'd made it clear she had ambitions and unlike most women, they didn't seem to include marriage or even a lover. Yet, he'd detected a latent sensuality in her, as yet so delicate it could be crushed by the slightest careless deed. And so far, all his dealings with her had appeared to be careless in the extreme even when he tried to make it up to her. As he reached out to tug on the bell-pull to summon Jefferson, he had an idea. Aunt Hannah had taken a special interest in the school and she knew Keziah had temporarily taken over from the schoolmistress. Miss Price, the governess to his three cousins, would soon be moving from Linderbourne to enjoy the healthy seaside air of Brighton and his aunt would need a new governess. Of course, it was possible she'd already appointed someone but if not, then he would suggest to her that Keziah should be given the opportunity. Of course, she was not qualified and still rather young, but Matthew was sure he could make a case for her enthusiasm and ambition. Violet, Rose and Blanche had not liked stuffy Miss Price and had frequently complained about her, so Aunt Hannah was pleased to see her go. Matthew was certain his three cousins would love Keziah and if he could persuade his aunt, it would be the perfect solution for everyone. It would remove Keziah from the unpleasant work she did in the mill, raise her to a position of governess and give her a fine home in Linderbourne Hall – a vast improvement on the Apprentice House. That would surely make up for any harm he'd inadvertently caused her in the past.

When Lucy learnt of the role Keziah had played in the previous night's attempt at ridding her of the threat of John Osgood, she'd be grateful to Keziah, who in time, might become a companion to Lucy. She was always complaining of the lack of suitable company and perhaps some common sense might rub off on his sister who needed to be reined in to prevent scandal in the future. Yes, it would be perfect for everyone.

And he would be able to see her when he liked.

During the walk from the Apprentice House to the mill, on Monday morning, Keziah felt sick. She'd forced down the unappetising breakfast into a stomach that was knotted and churning at the thought of seeing John Osgood again. She told herself repeatedly he wouldn't know her part in Saturday night's encounter.

How could he?

Nevertheless, it felt as though something might have given her away. Osgood, however, appeared to be distracted and was not even his usual brutal self. Later that day, he was called away for a meeting with Mr Rigby and she was allowed out early as usual in time to clean herself and change to go the schoolhouse. She was looking forward to the evening as Miss Maynard would be back and she anticipated spending time revealing some of the successes and a few of the failures of her time in charge.

But whereas she'd dreaded going to the mill and then found it had been much better than expected, when she arrived early at the schoolhouse, Miss Maynard greeted her with an angry outburst.

"So, I make an enormous effort to help you to prepare for advancement, but you couldn't wait! You had to push yourself forward in an unbecoming manner and snatch the one thing I wanted! Oh, don't look so innocent!" she said at Keziah's puzzled frown, "you know exactly to what I'm referring." She stood, hands on hips waiting for a reply.

At first, Keziah was so surprised, wondering if Miss Maynard had lost her reason, she didn't know what to say until she finally managed, "I... I... I'm sorry, Miss Maynard, I have no idea what you mean."

"Oh, don't add to your deceit by lying! You took advantage of my indisposition to ingratiate yourself with Mrs Rigby and to procure for yourself the post of governess! You! With no experience! While I, with so many years of teaching, have been cast aside. I had no idea you could be so unscrupulous and scheming!"

"But I—"

"Oh! Please don't attempt to explain your actions! It's obvious what you've done and I have been charged with giving you the good news. So, you are to return to the Apprentice House and collect your belongings. From tomorrow, you'll be living at Linderbourne Hall. I suspect you'll feel yourself much too grand to be mixing with the likes of simple folk like us!" Miss Maynard's face twisted with scorn. "Well, don't just stand there... Go!"

She dabbed her eyes and turned her face away from Keziah, indicating the interview was over.

"Please, Miss Maynard, there's obviously been a dreadful mistake..."

Miss Maynard held up her hand to silence her, "No mistake, I assure you," she picked up a letter from the desk and waved it angrily. "This is from Mrs Rigby and it is quite clear. You start your new position tomorrow morning in the Hall. Now, go!" She slowly crossed her arms and although her eyes had narrowed with anger, her chin was trembling.

Keziah looked around the schoolroom sadly. How could everything have gone so wrong? She'd longed for a position in a large house such as Linderbourne Hall but not like this. Not only had she lost the goodwill of the schoolmistress, but she'd been given a position for which she had no experience. As soon as that was discovered, she'd be dismissed. And what would happen to her then? Her hopes of offering Henry a stable home would be dashed. There was only one explanation. There'd been a dreadful mistake. But how had it happened?

Mrs Hagley had also received a letter informing her about Keziah's change in circumstances, and when Keziah awoke the following morning, several of the girls congratulated her with varying degrees of envy.

"Well done," said Becky without feeling, "I'll wager you can't wait to leave all this behind." She waved her hand vaguely at the dormitory and her sneer transformed itself into a smile, as her eyes alighted on the bed she'd no longer have to share.

During breakfast, Keziah tried to get Henry on his own to tell him but he'd been deep in conversation with Jack and although on several occasions she raised her eyebrows at him to ask how he was, she never managed to catch his eye. It was as if he was deliberately ignoring her. She decided she'd tell him during the walk to the mill but when she set out, she could find neither Henry nor Jack among the crowd.

Fearing being late on her first day, she dared not tarry. The mistake in engaging her would be discovered before long and she would be instantly dismissed, but no one would find fault in her time-keeping.

At the crossroads, Keziah stopped. Everyone else turned right towards the mill, moving around her swiftly and heedlessly, like water flowing past a rock in the Linderbourne River. She waited until everyone had gone but still, no Henry.

He wouldn't have deliberately avoided her, she was certain. Or would he? She realised she no longer knew.

Mrs Rigby received Keziah in the morning room. She sat with her back to the tall windows through which sunlight streamed. Keziah screwed up her eyes against the brightness as the mistress of Linderbourne Hall acknowledged her new governess's curtsey with a flourish of her hand.

With every movement, the colours of Mrs Rigby's high-necked silk robe and matching turban flashed in the sun's rays. She held a lorgnette to her face and peered at the girl with the small bag who was standing on the Oriental carpet. Keziah's heart sank as she took in the lips pressed tightly together in what appeared to be disappointment – or disapproval. This was not the start she'd hoped for, but it was the response she'd expected and feared.

Mrs Rigby sighed deeply. "Well, you come highly recommended and I must admit I was impressed when I saw you with the apprentices in the schoolhouse." As if trying to convince herself she'd made a good choice. "You are, of course, only here on trial. If you are as accomplished as I've been led to believe, your position will become permanent. My daughters are... well, shall we say... spirited. So, I must insist they are kept under control."

"Yes, ma'am," Keziah said, her voice quivering with apprehension.

"There's no need to feel overawed, my dear," Mrs Rigby said peering at her over the lorgnette, "I expect you'll do admirably." Her tone softened. "Well, I'll call Mary to help you take your belongings up to your room. Where are your other bags?"

Before Keziah could explain she had everything she owned in one bag, Mrs Rigby had rung a small handbell and seconds later, Mary arrived. Her eyes widened in surprise and at her knowing glance, Keziah blushed, remembering the day Matthew had called her to this very room and the serving girl had seen them both together.

"Miss Bonner?" Mrs Rigby tilted her head to one side, "Are you ill? You appear to be very flushed."

"I'm fine, thank you, ma'am."

"Excellent. Well, I'll make arrangements for you to have a bath immediately and for your clothes to be washed. I confess I find the smell of that dreadful oil they use on the mill machines quite offensive. It seems to cling to everyone who goes near it." She wrinkled her nose and dabbed at it with a handkerchief. "I'll have new clothes delivered to your room and they can be altered if necessary. You may spend the rest of the day settling in. We have guests arriving shortly so my daughters will be occupied. They will meet you in the schoolroom tomorrow at nine sharp. Do not be late. I do not tolerate tardiness. Mary will show you what you need to know and I will ensure she brings you supper in your room. Do you have any questions?"

"No, ma'am, thank you, ma'am." Keziah's cheeks burned with shame at learning her smell was so offensive to her new mistress that she was being ordered to have a bath.

Mary looked questioningly at the bag Keziah clutched to her chest and glanced at her mistress to see whether she should carry it upstairs, but Mrs Rigby had turned back to her breakfast. The interview was over. Mary shrugged imperceptibly and held the door open for Keziah, then led the way across the hall towards the grand staircase.

"The dining room's over there, the library's there, that's the music room and just past that is the master's study," she said, making no attempt to open the huge mahogany doors that led off the entrance hall and show Keziah the interiors. She chattered about members of the household as she limped up the main staircase and on the first landing, she pointed out three adjoining rooms, "The young ladies' rooms are here and your room is next to them. Miss Price, the last governess used the back stairs like the rest of us servants, unless she was with the young ladies, then she used the main staircase. Miss Price didn't put on airs and graces."

Keziah knew she was being warned not to behave as though she was better than Mary. After all, hadn't they both started as mill girls? For the first time Keziah became aware that in assuming this position which she'd once coveted, friendship with anyone she'd once mixed with was now impossible. She would now be resented by apprentices and servants alike but not accepted by the Rigby family. In short, she was entirely alone.

She remembered the words of the churchwarden at St Margaret's who'd told the children they would be trained to be ladies and gentlemen, to trick them into agreeing to go with Mr Rigby and therefore free up places in the workhouse. How naïve the children had been – and she'd been little better. She hadn't quite believed it but still, she'd hoped it was true, and she'd been happy to see Henry enthusiastic about the prospect of a new life.

Henry. A chill ran through her as she realised that while she was living in Linderbourne Hall, she wouldn't be able to keep an eye on him.

Not that he would mind. During the last few weeks while Jack's influence over him had increased, Henry had not appeared to think of his sister at all. She didn't believe he could have thrown off those years of devotion to each other so quickly. It wasn't possible. She suspected Henry was once again hiding his true feelings behind a mask of deception. He was flattered at the older boy's attention and perhaps even attracted by the excitement.

She knew being locked in the dark storeroom for hours had deeply disturbed him and at first, she'd assumed his fear of the darkness would curtail his nightly expeditions with Jack but that had not proved to be so.

Although the woods were dark and forbidding and still made her shiver at the thought of them, she could see how they were nothing like that tiny room in which Henry had once been locked. When she'd learnt what had happened to him and how he'd developed a fear of confined, dark spaces, the rage had blazed inside her until it reached white heat – he was her brother and she'd been unable to keep him safe. Those who'd been put in charge of his care had harmed him and she would never forgive them for the scars they'd heedlessly inflicted on a small boy. Men such as Mr Clegg would always have her utter contempt. She'd often wondered if Henry would grow out of his fear of the dark. Perhaps his regular trips into the woods weren't such a bad thing – or they wouldn't have been if they hadn't carried the threat of being caught and charged with poaching. But whatever was going on in Henry's mind now, he didn't share with her and now she was several miles away, there would be nothing she could do to help him should he need her.

"Here," said Mary breaking into Keziah's thoughts. She opened a door into a pale-yellow bedroom, "this is your'n. Me and Gracie will prepare your bath, ma'am," Mary said although it was obvious from the way she hesitated before adding 'ma'am' that she wasn't sure the difference between them was great enough to use such a polite form of address.

While Keziah waited for Mary's return she looked around her new room. How wonderful to have a bed to herself. And what a bed! It was several times larger than the one she'd shared with Becky, with a thick mattress and linen hangings that matched the curtains and cushions on the window seat. A washstand with china basin and ewer stood next to a chest of drawers and a full-length mirror – and they were all hers. Not for long, admittedly but at least she might as well enjoy them while she could.

There was a tap at the door and when she opened it, two footmen carrying a copper bath entered and placed it in front of the fireplace. Seconds after, Mary and several other maids arrived with steaming jugs of water which they tipped into the bath, leaving with a promise of more water and fresh clothes.

"Mrs Rigby says I'm to take your clothes immediately and if they're too bad, I'm to burn 'em," said Mary, her cheeks flushed and her gaze lowered as if she couldn't meet Keziah's eyes. "Don't take it personal... it's just that Mrs Rigby can't stand the smell of us mill girls."

There it was. Mary still thought of them both as mill girls. As if they were tainted. And yet, Keziah knew enough about the apprentices to realise that having lifted themselves above the mill workers, neither she nor Mary would ever be accepted back. Perhaps Mary, with her lame leg might be forgiven for having left the mill but Keziah would never be excused for having the audacity to try to better herself – something most of the apprentices would have done if they'd had the opportunity.

Keziah stripped off and climbed into the bath. Soap and towels had been left for her and she began to scrub herself energetically. Gradually, the lavender-laden steam filled her nostrils, cleaning away the smell of the familiar machine oil. She lathered her hair vigorously, grateful for the ample supply of soap – a commodity that hadn't been readily available in the Apprentice House. When she'd finished, Mary arrived with more clothes over her arm and another jug of hot water which she poured into the bath.

As Mary handed Keziah a towel, she had a flashback to a beautiful room and a maid who'd arrived with new clothes for her sister, Eva, so many years before.

"Are you all right, miss?" Mary asked, catching sight of Keziah's shocked expression.

"Yes, yes I just remembered something that happened a long time ago."

"Something that weren't a good memory?"

Keziah nodded. "Not a good memory at all. In fact, my life was never the same after that day."

Mary shifted from one foot to the other as if not sure what to say to this girl who'd started out in the mill like her but was now her superior. "Oh, I don't know," she said, forcing a cheery voice, "you caught the eye of Mr Gregory and that done you good so perhaps your life ain't so bad."

"Mr Gregory?" Keziah's cheeks reddening as she stuttered a denial. "I assure you I have not caught his eye. He called me here the other day because he believed I had some information for him."

"No, I weren't talking about when you came here," said Mary. "I heard you scolding him. No, I meant the governess's job. Mrs Rigby had it in mind to offer it to Miss Maynard but it was Mr Gregory what persuaded her to give it to you."

Matthew? Of course, it could only have been he who'd recommended her to his aunt. Mrs Rigby had mentioned being impressed when she'd seen Keziah teach the apprentices but she'd also said 'You come highly recommended...' The only person who was in a position to have recommended her was Miss Maynard but after their earlier conversation, Keziah knew without doubt, it wasn't her. So, it must have been Matthew. Tears of fury pricked her eyes. Foolish, foolish man! Why couldn't he just leave her alone? Since he'd burst into the schoolroom and her life, he'd caused her problem after problem.

The Rigby's guests arrived in a smart carriage and later, Keziah saw the ladies in their beautiful gowns strolling through the gardens and their laughter drifted up to her. She sat on the window seat, her arms wrapped around her knees and her chin resting on top as she observed the gaiety below. Destined to watch, but never to participate.

Later, she heard music and singing, followed by more chatter and laughter and the chink of cutlery against plates. The steady tick-tock of the clock on the mantelpiece seemed to grow louder and louder, filling the room, while the colourful curtains and green wallpaper-clad walls appeared to close in. Despite the lavish surroundings, she felt as though she were in prison.

Why had Matthew interfered? If only she'd never met him!

Tick-tock.

Tick-tock.

Keziah yawned.

She wished she had a book or something to do, but she dared not venture out of her room and risk running into any of the Rigby family or their guests. There was so much she didn't know. Would she be allowed to borrow a book from the library? Would she even be permitted to go in there? But now she thought about it, she couldn't remember which of the doors Mary had told her led into which room. It wouldn't do to blunder into Mr Rigby's study instead of the library or music room.

Mary brought her supper and she ate alone while the sun dipped behind the crest of the hill. How much more enjoyable the meal would have been if it had been shared – the mutton and vegetables, followed by gooseberry cream had been delicious but she'd have forgone the entire meal for a bowl of thin bacon soup and black bread with the others in the Apprentice House.

When her plates had been removed, Keziah decided to go to bed. It was much too early to sleep but this was a day she was eager to forget and the sooner she was in bed, the sooner she'd be lost to her dreams.

She removed the pins from her hair and allowed the curls to tumble around her shoulders, then roughly pulled the comb through them, tugging until she brought tears to her eyes. In truth, the tears were not far away from welling up on their own accord. She glared at herself in the mirror, furious because her hopes for the future had been realised in a way that she had not foreseen. But how could anyone have predicted this? There should have been a logical progression over months or perhaps years while she gained more experience. Then, when she was ready, she'd hoped Miss Maynard would recommend her for a less responsible post and, given time, she'd have worked her way into a position such as the one she now held. She'd be confident and she'd make a success of it. Finally, she'd provide a family home for Henry and then... Well, what did it matter what happened after that? They would be master and mistress of their own lives. Beholden to no one.

But now because of the interference of a spoilt, rich, young man, she had a job she didn't deserve – a post that should have gone to Miss Maynard. The woman who felt betrayed by the girl she'd favoured and encouraged.

While Mary had shown Keziah the schoolroom, she'd mentioned that the Hall was filled with music on Wednesdays when the three Misses Rigby learnt dancing and music – subjects about which Keziah knew nothing. Her cheeks burned each time she imagined the conversation with Mrs Rigby when she discovered her new governess's lack of accomplishments.

Of course, it wouldn't have occurred to Matthew she hadn't received the same level of education as someone of his social standing. Nevertheless, he'd set her up for humiliation.

The comb caught in a particularly tangled curl and she tugged at it angrily. Tomorrow she'd be dismissed. She'd be sent back to the Apprentice House to resume her work in the mill.

And Henry? What would he think? Would he even care?

She stared at herself in the mirror, her face white and tense. How had it come to this? How could her life have gone so wrong?

There was a tap at the door.

"Come!" she said wondering what it was Mary wanted now. The servant had knocked several times, bringing items of clothing that had been altered for her. As she turned to the door, the comb still caught in a particularly knotted tangle, she idly wondered what would happen to those clothes that had been sewn to fit her, when she was sent back to the Apprentice House in disgrace.

To her shock, it wasn't Mary who opened the door and stepped inside her room, it was Matthew Gregory.

Keziah tried to pull the comb out of her hair but it was stuck fast and, in her confusion, she pulled it out with such force, several hairs came out of her scalp and once again tears sprang to her eyes. She put the comb down quickly and stood up.

He should not be in her room.

But this was his uncle's house. Presumably, he could do as he pleased. Her cheeks flamed with embarrassment at being seen with a comb caught in her unpinned hair but at least, it fell forward slightly hiding her red face. How fortunate she was still dressed, even if she was barefoot.

His face lit up with a conspiratorial smile. "I trust you're settling in well?"

It was phrased as a question but he didn't seem to expect an answer as if he couldn't believe it possible she might not be settling in well in such a luxurious setting.

How self-satisfied he looked.

"I know my cousins will adore you when they meet you tomorrow," he said.

Embarrassment fuelled the anger that was burning inside.

Did he expect her to express undying gratitude at his magnanimous gesture?

Or did he want more? He'd promised anything that happened in the Other Place would remain there but had he taken their kiss as a sign that she would do whatever he asked? She was in a world she knew nothing about – perhaps people behaved differently?

Well, whatever the reason, she would let him know she owed him nothing. She strode across the bedroom towards him and for the first time, his smile faltered as he caught sight of her narrowed eyes and determined expression.

"So, you're certain your cousins will adore me, are you? Well, it's such a pity then, your aunt is unlikely to keep me here long enough for them to find out! Why can't you leave me alone and stop meddling in my life?" Her voice was harsh and shrill and he took a step backwards, away from her forefinger that jabbed the air inches from his chest.

After a moment of shock, his eyebrows drew together as if he was hurt.

Hurt?

He knew nothing about being hurt! How dare he assume such a pained expression!

"I... I don't understand," he stammered. "I thought you wanted—"

"You thought? But that's just it, you didn't think! The problem is you have no idea about my life or how I need to live it."

"But your dream—"

"I think the word you need to consider there is 'Your'. It was *my* dream and I am now about to see it broken into tiny pieces!"

"But why? You'll be perfect!"

"Perfect? I'm not ready! I have no idea how to teach young ladies how to dance nor to play the piano and I expect I'll be required to teach them French and painting... and how to be young ladies... These are things I have no idea how to do, and you've put me in a position where my shortcomings will be obvious to your aunt and I'll be discharged without references. You've ruined my life!" She gasped for breath in what sounded suspiciously like a sob and stared at him silently, knowing if she tried to say anything, her voice would give away how close she was to crying.

He opened his mouth to speak, then closed it again and took a step away from her. With his hand on the latch, he said softly, "I see this new post has been a lot for you to take in and I'm going to assume you are overwhelmed. But, you will be perfect, I know. There is no need for you to teach my cousins French, painting, dancing or music. Tutors come each week from the town to teach them those subjects. You are here to ensure they have a basic knowledge of reading, writing and arithmetic exactly as you teach the children in the mill school. You will be there to take them for walks and keep them from under my aunt's feet. I do not believe it will overburden you. However, if I have yet again interfered in your life and caused problems, I sincerely beg your pardon." He nodded briefly, "I bid you good night, Miss Bonner." He went out of the door and closed it softly.

She did not hear him walk along the hall immediately and she wondered whether her ears were misleading her or whether he was still outside. He'd been so calm and she knew she ought to apologise for her rudeness. But the rage that had consumed her could not be extinguished so quickly. It would be a while before she calmed down and could think rationally. It would also be a while before she would be composed enough to sleep.

Much later, Keziah sat on the window seat, gazing through the open window into the valley. The sun had set, the shadows had lengthened and the sky had deepened its hue yet, there was enough light to see the silhouette of the forest and the chimneys of the Apprentice House peeping above. She wondered where Henry was – safe inside the house or out with Jack Lawley? The curtains fluttered in the evening breeze and she shivered as the chilly air penetrated her thin nightgown but at least it had cooled her anger, leaving her feeling drained and deeply regretful. Again and again, she'd gone over what had happened when Matthew had come to her room and as her rage had subsided, she'd begun to view things differently. Initially, she'd seen self-satisfaction and conceit in Matthew's expression but now, she wondered if she'd been mistaken and what she'd seen had been his pleasure and a shared joy that she'd achieved what he believed was her dream. No one could reasonably argue he'd acted selfishly. He'd stood to gain nothing. No, it had been entirely for her benefit. He'd told her he wouldn't return to London but she doubted that and as soon as he'd gone, he wouldn't give her another thought – yet he had attempted to do something kind for her and in her embarrassment and pride, she'd rejected his help. And worse – she buried her face in her hands with shame at the memory – she'd repeatedly poked her finger at him, drawing short of actually prodding his chest, that same chest whose contours her hands had explored not long before with such keenness.

When it was too dark to see the Apprentice House chimneys, she climbed into the enormous bed, sliding between the sheets while her thoughts tumbled over and over. Memories of the kiss in that Other Place, her furious outburst earlier, her longing to see Matthew and her desire to apologise. Of course, she told herself, she only yearned to see him so she could beg his pardon...

The single chime of the church clock proclaimed it was one o'clock and still Keziah lay awake, dreading what the new day would bring. Despite discovering she wouldn't be expected to teach dancing, music and painting, she still wasn't confident in her abilities to satisfy Mrs Rigby. But if Matthew was correct and she was expected to ensure the Misses Rigby learnt arithmetic, reading and writing like the children in the mill school, perhaps she might keep the post for a day or two – long enough to try to form a plan. Although, if she didn't get to sleep soon, she wouldn't be able to keep her eyes open.

She was beginning to nod off when a scuffling at the door caught her attention. She propped herself on her elbow, listening intently and wondering if such a grand house had rats.

Had she dreamt it? She was about to lay down when she heard the rustling of clothes and creak of a floorboard outside in the hall, followed by a swish as if something had been pushed under the door. She sat up and straining to see in the blackness, she made out a pale rectangle against the dark floor.

Keziah scrambled out of bed and picked up the paper. It was too dark to read but she didn't need to see the writing to know it was from Matthew as the faint tang of sandalwood had wafted into the air when she'd unfolded the paper.

Opening the door, she looked left along the hall towards the stairs but there was no one there. She looked to the right, and there he was, silhouetted like a statue in the moonlight that was shining through the window at the end of the hall. He rocked forward for an instant as if about to walk away, then pausing as if acknowledging he'd been seen, he crept back towards her.

He softly cleared his throat. "I beg your pardon, I had no intention of waking you."

"It is of no matter, I could not sleep."

"Ah," he said sadly, then with what she recognised as forced joviality, he added, "I expect, like everything else that ails you, your sleeplessness is my fault."

"No, not at all. In fact... the... the fault is entirely mine." Why was it so hard to utter the words 'I am sorry?' In the past, her anger had been directed at those in charge – the parish authorities in the workhouse, the overlookers in the mill – and they deserved her scorn. If she'd managed to hide her feelings, her fury had simply burned inside and no one had known. If she hadn't managed to conceal it, she'd been punished. But she'd been the only victim. This time, she'd hurt someone else and he deserved to know she was sorry.

"I see," he said slowly as if waiting for further explanation but when she didn't speak, he added, "Well, I'm intrigued to know what it is you've done and I would help if I could but I know you don't welcome my interference."

Still, she remained silent and as he turned to leave, she knew there wouldn't be another opportunity to speak to him on his own. This was the perfect time to make amends – possibly the only chance she'd have. She forced the words out, "Please wait! I... I must speak with you."

He stopped and turned back to her, his brows drawn together. "May I come into your bedroom? It will not go well for either of us if we're seen like this."

Keziah stood back and allowed him in, aware for the first time she was merely wearing a nightshift. Mrs Rigby had ensured her new governess had several day frocks, a smart outfit for Sunday and a nightshift but she had not provided a dressing gown to cover it. However, it was dark in her bedroom, the only light, a ruby glow from the embers in the grate.

She would apologise and he would leave. There would not be time for him to notice what she was wearing – or not wearing.

Although the guests had left hours before and the house was now quiet, he'd obviously not retired, as he was still dressed. The faintest hint of brandy told her what he'd been doing, yet it could not have been to excess because his voice was clear and he walked steadily.

He hesitated in the doorway. "If you merely wish to tell me how much I vex you and to jab your finger at me again, perhaps we could continue this conversation tomorrow?"

"No," she said softly, unsure whether he was serious or not, "On the contrary, I'm vexed with myself for my rudeness and I wanted to beg your pardon."

"Truly?" He frowned as if not certain whether to believe her. "And what changed your opinion?"

"I... I..."

*Stop stammering and say the words! The longer you wait, the more embarrassing it will be.*

"I fear it's a failing of mine," she said quickly and then realising the force she'd used to prise out the words had made them louder than she'd intended and she was horrified as they echoed along the hall. Looking right and left to ensure no one had appeared to investigate the noise, he gestured they should go into her room and having closed the door softly, he stood opposite her – she on one side of the rug and he on the other.

Well, she'd started, so, she might as well continue with the humiliation and then, perhaps her conscience would be clear. She carried on in a whisper, "It is a failing of mine and if I believe I'm being treated unfairly or I'm afraid, I lose my temper. After I'd reflected on everything, I recognised your kindness... I wouldn't want you to believe I wasn't extremely grateful for attempting to help me."

"I see... You said if you're treated unfairly or if you're afraid, of which am I guilty?" He seemed genuinely confused.

"I... I was afraid."

"Of me?" His voice was a whisper and he shook his head in disbelief.

"No!"

"Then what? I've rarely met anyone with more spirit than you. So, what is it you fear?"

"Not being good enough. Of failing. I'm fearful of letting Henry down." The words came out in a rush and she hung her head so he couldn't see her shame. Never before had she apologised for her temper nor confessed she'd been afraid. It showed weakness. It handed someone the power to cause her pain.

So, why had she told Matthew Gregory?

"I, therefore, humbly beg your pardon, for my appalling rudeness," she said quickly, hoping to distract him. She'd apologised. Now he would leave.

But he didn't.

And perversely, she was glad.

They stared at each other over the rug, in the red glow of the firelight.

*Say something.*

*Say anything or he'll leave.*

*He ought to leave.*

*Yet...*

"The note!" they said in unison and both laughed.

*Had he been thinking of an excuse to stay?*

"What did you want to tell me?" she asked

"Ah, well... I too, wanted to apologise but I thought I'd done that so often, you'd find it tedious. Then I thought I'd try to be helpful but that usually results in me causing you a problem. So, in the end, I settled on some advice."

"And what do you advise?"

"I thought it would be useful for you to know that Blanche is the ringleader of the three sisters, and if you win her over, Violet and Rose will follow her lead. She's a girl who knows her own mind. Very much like her new governess. She's very bright but she becomes bored if she's required to sit still for any length of time. Miss Price insisted the girls sat in the schoolroom for hours reciting facts. I'm sure you can do better than that."

"Thank you... I... I don't know what to say... That was very good of you, considering my behaviour towards you."

"Good?" he asked in mock indignation, "Merely good? I'd say, it was saintly, at the very least, considering I came under attack from a finger that I suspect might well have been lethal, had it struck home!"

"You're laughing at me!" She looked up at him, surprised that she'd told him so much about herself and that she didn't mind him teasing her.

"A little, perhaps. Now, tell me, does that go some way towards allaying your fears and allowing you to sleep? Or is there something else worrying you?" He stepped onto the carpet, his hands raised, palms upwards as if he wanted to offer her something but didn't know what.

"I... I don't know what to say, you've been so thoughtful and it seems ungrateful, but... while I'm here, I will no longer be able to keep an eye on Henry."

Matthew paused and dropped his hands to his side. "Unfortunately, tomorrow, my uncle has demanded I meet with him and discuss my affairs. I don't anticipate the interview will go well and it depends on his generosity as to what happens then. He may insist Lucy and I remain here where he can supervise us – well, at least until my father dies after which time, I'll inherit everything and will be able to do as I please. Or he may not want us under his roof and send us back to London. Before he grows too angry – and rest assured, he will be furious – I'll ask if he needs another footman. And if he does, then Henry will be here and you'll be able to keep an eye on him."

"You'd do that for me?" Keziah pressed her fingers to her lips, hardly able to believe his words. She took a step towards him.

"Didn't you help me with my sister?"

"But..." She paused, having been about to say she'd spent years in service to people of Matthew's class but they never thought to do her a kindness. That would have been churlish. Instead, she said, "I couldn't in all conscience have allowed you to appear dressed as a woman – even to John Osgood." She smiled mischievously.

He took another step towards her and raised her chin with his finger, "How cruel you are." His voice was playful. Teasing.

He was so close now, she could smell brandy on his breath and hints of sandalwood warmed by his body heat escaping from the open neck of his shirt.

His smile faded. "But I don't want to raise your hopes. My uncle is likely to be too furious with me to listen to my request for Henry."

"Why will he be furious?"

"I scarcely know where to start." He took a half-step backwards and ran his fingers through his hair. "But, since you have been honest with me, I shall tell you. I have spent the last few years seeking excitement and pleasure and in so doing, have run up large debts. My uncle, thus far, has reluctantly covered my bills but there will come a time when he no longer feels under obligation to pay and then... well, perhaps it'll be the debtors' prison. And before you ask why I don't simply stop my extravagant lifestyle, I fully intend to. However, I have several creditors who require payment now and when Uncle sees the extent of what I owe, he may refuse to pay. I will assure him I have changed, but I've done that three times before with no intention of doing so. This time, he can hardly be blamed for not believing me. Tomorrow, I will admit to all the money that I owe before he is presented with the bills, and in that way, I hope to demonstrate my intention to change. But it is such a large sum to have squandered..."

"He will believe you, I'm sure."

"You wouldn't say that if you knew some of the foolish things I've done. I've lost a fortune at the gaming tables and the races. I've drunk until I couldn't remember where I lived or who I was. My apology to Uncle Obadiah tomorrow must be convincing indeed." He paused and as if talking himself out of his despair, he added lightly, "I don't wish to criticise, but my speech tomorrow must be a sight more convincing and heartfelt than your apology earlier."

94

"Are you saying," she said with mock outrage, "that mine was in any way inadequate?"

He tipped his head on one side, pretending to consider. "Well, I'd say there could have been slightly more grovelling involved. Or persuasion... yes, indeed, persuasion might have assisted your apology, your rather *poor* apology, if I may say so, Miss Bonner."

"Perhaps I ought to try again, Mr Gregory?"

"Hmm... You could try... but take heed, you will need to be very persuasive indeed."

"And how do you propose I do that?"

"I need to look into your eyes to judge your commitment. And I need to do this..." He stepped closer to her and took her hands. "Self-defence. A precaution against you poking me again."

"I did not poke you earlier! I didn't touch you!"

"True, but how do I know you won't be tempted to start? In the Other Place, anything can happen."

"Is that where we are?"

"I believe so. Don't you?"

"Yes," her voice was breathless, quivering with fear and anticipation.

This was madness, she knew, but anything that happened from this point on would signify nothing. It was a game. Mere pretence. And she knew he wouldn't do anything she didn't want.

Or did she? Hadn't she always lived her life knowing people were selfish and would use her for their own ends? But in the Other Place, there were no expectations and there would be no repercussions. It would be an experiment. She wanted to hold his hand. She wanted to feel his lips against hers again. Just this once.

"Well, Mr Gregory, I really must apologise for my behaviour."

He tilted his head to one side and looked upwards pretending to consider. "No, I'm sorry, I'm still not convinced. I fear it may take more than words. Perhaps if you came closer...?"

He placed his hands on her shoulders and she could feel their warmth through the thin lawn of her nightshift. "Yes," he whispered that seems to be working. I'm feeling very warmly disposed towards you, Miss Bonner. In fact, I'm finding it hard to remember why an apology is necessary." His hands glided down her back to her waist and pulled her closer.

"I believe, Mr Gregory, it may have had something to do with my finger almost touching your chest."

Dare she?

Why not? The next time they met, it would be as Mr Rigby's nephew and the lowly governess. Now, in the Other Place, they were equals. Simply a man and a woman.

She placed the pad of one finger on his chest and gently moved it across the fabric of his shirt towards the V-shaped area of bare skin.

He moaned softly and as she'd hoped, leaned towards her and placed his lips over hers. As she slid her hands up to link around his neck, he abruptly took them in his and breaking away from her, he held them to his lips. The disappointment in her face must have been obvious because he said, "This is for the best. Trust me. I must prove I can be honourable – to my uncle, to you and to myself. And when I've done that, we won't need the Other Place. The real world will be our Other Place."

He pressed her hands to his lips again, then to his cheek and turned on his heel and left.

She couldn't believe he'd gone. And what did he mean 'the real world will be our Other Place?' It wasn't possible. At least now, her conscience was clear – she'd apologised to him for her earlier rudeness. But how disappointing he'd left her like that, although, she acknowledged, it was probably just as well he'd kept his head because for the first time ever, she realised she'd temporarily lost all reason and who knew where that might have led?

The following morning, Keziah was ready and waiting for Mrs Rigby and her three daughters when they entered the schoolroom. Her stomach was knotted with nerves and it lurched as they walked in; she hoped she looked more awake than she felt. Before leaving her room, she'd splashed her face repeatedly with cold water and it had helped but her eyes were gritty and red-rimmed with lack of sleep.

Mrs Rigby introduced her three daughters and explained what she required: "I want you to teach my daughters the skills they needed to become educated and well-mannered young ladies and I am relying on you, Miss Bonner."

"Yes, ma'am, I shall endeavour to do my best."

"Then I shall leave you to your work." She frowned at the girls who smiled back innocently and then she hurried out of the schoolroom leaving Keziah in charge.

It seemed to be as Matthew had suggested. The twins, Violet and Rose copied everything their elder sister did and with dismay, Keziah recognised the disrespect in Blanche's eyes. She appeared to be assessing the new governess and from working with Miss Maynard, Keziah knew the first moments would be crucial in determining the behaviour of the sisters. She must be bold and unpredictable.

"Thank you girls. Now, I'm going to tell you a secret," Keziah said once the girls had finally settled down.

That caught their attention.

"Is it a secret about you, Miss Bonner?" Blanche asked.

"It's a secret about all of us."

Three faces looked at her expectantly.

"I'd like you to imagine what your lives will be like in the future... Now consider what you'll need to know in order to live that life..."

"You mean something like managing a house as Mama does?" Violet asked.

"Or sewing?" Rose screwed up her face in distaste.

"Or being with child?" Blanche asked feigning innocence.

"Blanche!" The twins gasped at their sister's boldness, then began to giggle.

"I mean all of those things," Keziah said ignoring Blanche's blatant attempt to shock her.

"So, what is the secret, Miss Bonner?" Blanche asked.

"Simply this. Determine whatever you think you will need to equip you for the future. Then, tell yourself you're likely to be entirely wrong."

The girls looked at her in surprise.

"Your lives are very unlikely to become what you imagine."

"How do you know?" Violet asked.

"Ask any of your family if their lives have turned out as they expected."

"Why are you telling us this?" Blanche tipped her head to one side.

"Well done, Blanche. I can see you're a girl who thinks things through carefully..."

"Oh!" Blanche smiled with pride.

"I'm telling you all because if you can't control what happens to you, you can at least make sure you're prepared for all eventualities."

"How do you do that?"

"You take every opportunity to learn as much as you can. All information is useful because you never know when you'll need it. The only protection you have from whatever befalls you is to understand about it and to turn the situation to your advantage." Keziah wasn't sure it was what Mrs Rigby wanted her daughters to learn, but at least, she had piqued their interest and with any luck, the girls would try harder at their lessons. It would be up to her to make those lessons interesting and different but at least for the time being, they were on her side.

"Where did you think you'd be when you were my age, Miss Bonner?" Blanche asked but this time, her tone was respectful and full of interest.

"I grew up in London. My father owned a watchmakers' shop and when I was younger than you, I wanted to marry, Jacob, one of Papa's apprentices. I assumed my life would be similar to my mother's. But, as you can see, that didn't happen..." She would tell them enough of her life to illustrate her point. One tiny part. The shame of how she'd betrayed Eva and was currently letting Henry down, would remain her secret.

Against all odds, the rest of the day passed relatively well. Blanche had taken to Keziah and therefore, so had the twins. They were lively, intelligent girls and Keziah knew she would be heartbroken when Mrs Rigby decided she wasn't good enough to teach her daughters.

That night, to her surprise and delight, Matthew returned to her room to ask about her day and to save them being seen, she invited him in. He stood awkwardly on one side of the rug, the informality of the night before had gone. She wondered if he'd had more brandy the previous evening than she'd realised. He'd been more relaxed than he was now. How could they resume the ease they'd experienced? She longed to continue where they'd left off...

"If we were in the Other Place, I'd invite you to sit..." She left the sentence hanging and gestured to the window seat.

He smiled at her. "And if you invited me, I'd gratefully accept. It would be good to speak to someone who wasn't angry with me..." He paused and added, "you're not angry with me, are you?" His smile was mischievous and she knew he was teasing. She deserved such treatment. Since she'd met him, hadn't she alternated between being furious with him and then captivated by him in some strange heady mixture she didn't understand? How could he know whether her temper might suddenly erupt?

Keziah was glad she'd indicated the window seat rather than the two hard-backed chairs. It wasn't very comfortable, but at least, they were sitting side by side, his arm touching hers. He turned and took her hand, then with his face inches from hers, he told her about the meeting with his uncle. Keziah had feared the worst because as she and the girls had passed the study earlier on their way to the library, she'd heard Mr Rigby shouting, his words punctuated by the thumping of a fist on the desk. She'd hurried the girls along but they'd all heard Mr Rigby thundering the words 'profligate', 'rake' and 'ingrate', before they were out of earshot.

"I've never seen him so livid." Matthew sighed. "I truly thought he'd wash his hands of me."

"And? Did he?" She held her breath, not wanting to hear he'd be sent back to London in disgrace.

"Thankfully, no. I gave him my solemn oath I'd work hard to pay him back. He didn't believe me at first but eventually, thanks to you, I managed to convince him—"

"Thanks to me?"

"Yes, no need to sound so surprised. I've never met anyone who has such ambition. None of my friends looks further than the next social event. Their wealth has been passed down through the generations and even if it's now beginning to dwindle, there's always the expectation things will get better. But you have no such expectations. You're determined to force things to improve. And I need to do the same. So, I came up with an idea that pleased Uncle. I'd already suggested I go into business with him but I needed more."

"What did you suggest?"

"I remembered Uncle saying he's looking for more land to build another village and mill. I've agreed to go into business with him and when I inherit my father's estates, I'll provide the land and he'll bring his expertise. It's a perfect solution." Matthew paused, then turned to look out of the window.

"And yet, you don't seem happy."

He sighed. "Not entirely... It's a big step and if my father knew, he'd forbid it."

"But why?"

"Because he despises trade. I know that may appear strange since his estates have been losing money for years and if he'd followed Uncle Obadiah's example, he'd probably be worth a fortune, but... well, it's complicated. The prejudice runs deep amongst people of my class. Aunt Hannah is my father's sister and he forbade her to marry Uncle Obadiah. Not that my uncle isn't from a good family but he'd committed the sin of going into business and in Father's eyes, he'd lost his dignity and his position in society. They married secretly. Of course, London society was shocked and one particular man insulted both Aunt Hannah and her new husband, leaving Father no alternative but to challenge him to a duel."

"A duel!" Keziah was about to add, 'how foolish', but thought better of it. Of course, she knew the practice went on amongst the upper class but how much simpler to settle disputes with a punch on the nose like the people with whom she usually mixed. Instead, she asked what had happened.

"Father and his opponent were both slightly injured but the following day, my father suffered an apoplectic fit. After some months, he recovered his speech and some movement but he's never been the same. And that's why Uncle Obadiah feels an obligation to Father – and to Lucy and me. But he won't feel obligated forever. So, like you, I need a plan for my future and that's why I've decided to join him... despite knowing it would upset my father deeply if he were to find out. But then..." He shrugged and turned to face her. "As I seem to be incapable of pleasing my father, at least I won't be a disappointment. I shall simply be living down to his expectations."

"Oh, Matthew!" Her voice caught in her throat. How sad he looked. Defeated.

With a slight shake of his head as if to throw off such miserable thoughts, he smiled and said, "No need to fret." He took her other hand and held them both to his lips. "This will free me to do what I want – to be me. And once I'm my own person, the Other Place will become real. And when it does, you and I can really be together."

Keziah pulled her hands from his in alarm. "No! Pray don't say such things! Not even in jest. The Other Place may become real for you but it never will for me. It will always be somewhere I have to pretend to be better than I am."

"But that isn't true! You've told me about your family they were from the middling sort. Had your parents lived, you'd have probably been fairly wealthy."

"Had my parents lived, that may have been true. But they didn't." She shook her head and tried to keep the tears in check. "And now, my belongings are so few, I can pack them in one bag."

"But I care nothing for that! Once we're married, I would give you anything—"

"Married! No, please stop!" She reached out and placed a finger over his lips. Had he been drinking after all? He certainly seemed sober but surely he was muddling reality and fantasy. "In the Other Place, anything can happen but not in the real world. We could never marry! I had no thought of such a thing! I have to look after Henry. Please don't mention this again. There are so many reasons why it would be a bad idea, I can hardly list them!"

"I know my proposal is very sudden and we haven't known each other long but I've never been more certain of anything. You've filled my thoughts night and day since I first met you. And I know that together, we could overcome—"

"No! Don't you see? It's impossible! And even if we could be together, I'd only hurt you. I'm too headstrong. I destroy everything of value in my life. I don't mean to be but—"

"I know you have a vicious finger," he said, mimicking her jabbing at his chest. He smiled, his eyes pleading with her to join in with his joke.

"Please listen to me, I'm being serious—"

He sighed. "What you're being, Keziah, is melodramatic. I know of no one kinder nor more loyal. It's true we've only known each other a short while but I've never felt so sure of anyone. I love you, Keziah! You must know that. Ever since I've met you, I've wanted to help you, to protect you. And yes, I know I got everything wrong but that wasn't my intention. I thought you felt the same..." He put a finger under her chin and tilted her face up so he could look into her eyes. "I beg you, if you don't feel the same about me, tell me now and I'll leave you alone."

Keziah stared at him for several seconds. How easy it would be to fall into his arms now. But they would never be allowed to be together. It was nonsense. Tempting, so tempting, but impossible.

"Please..." he whispered, emotion choking his voice.

It was up to her to be strong. "I will tell you." She took a deep breath. "The truth is, I ruin everything I touch. It's better that you know this now. I've told you about my family and how we lost everything..." her eyes narrowed as she remembered her father's callous business partner, "I haven't told you about my elder sister, Eva."

He looked at her questioningly. "I didn't know you had a sister. Where is she?"

"By now, almost certainly dead and buried halfway across the world. She was wrongfully convicted of a crime I committed and she was transported for seven years. After that, I vowed to take care of Henry and to provide him with a home. And that must be my focus."

"But what happened?" he asked softly, taking her hands again.

"Our aunt had turned us out and we found ourselves with a dreadful woman who took me out stealing. She threatened to hurt Henry if I didn't help her, so I distracted people while she picked their pockets. Eva told me not to call the constable. She also told me we'd be separated from Henry if we went to the parish and told them we were homeless. But would I listen? No! I always know best! But it turned out, I knew nothing. I called a constable and when he wanted to arrest me, Eva took my place. I never saw her again. And of course, she was right about being separated from Henry in the workhouse. So, you see. I broke my family apart with my pride." The lump in her throat grew too large to carry on but indeed, what more was there to say?

Matthew squeezed her hands but held on to them when she tried to draw them away. "You could only have been a child yourself when that happened."

She nodded, unable to speak as the memories flooded back of seeing Eva dragged away by the constable, of kicking and biting the man who held her to try to get to her sister and of being overcome and taken to St Margaret's Workhouse.

"You can't be held responsible for not knowing how the world works. Nor of trying to do your best..." he said, lifting her chin and looking into her eyes.

"I ruin everything. You'll be happier with someone of your own class who understands your world – the real world – not the Other Place which, as we both know, doesn't exist. Please Matthew, if you love me as you say you do, you'll forget me. You now have your dream, even if you aren't completely convinced it's what you want. And I must do what I can to make things up to Henry." She bit her bottom lip and hoped the pain would stop her tears. "And anyway, I don't love you." The lie cut through her like a knife but it was the only way she could ensure he wouldn't try to persuade her.

He tenderly kissed her forehead, then left her. She'd convinced him and she knew with all her heart it was over. The heart that had just broken in two.

Early on Friday, Keziah was summoned to the morning room. It was most alarming because Mrs Rigby had given Keziah seven days to prove herself, telling her that on Tuesday sennight she'd be required to discuss the girls' progress. So far, she thought her attempts to teach the girls had been remarkably successful. Nevertheless, it now appeared she hadn't even lasted one week in the post. She could taste the bitterness rising at the back of her throat.

"Ah, Miss Bonner, punctual as usual," said Mrs Rigby, dabbing the corners of her mouth with a napkin. She paused, studying the contents of her cup as if unable to make eye contact. Finally, she cleared her throat. "I'm afraid I have some bad news for you."

Keziah hung her head, her cheeks hot with shame. Why didn't she simply dismiss her and be done?

Mrs Rigby placed her napkin on the table and stared at it. "I'm afraid my husband has just been informed of an attack on one of the mill overlookers."

Keziah had been bracing herself for words such as 'dismissed', 'unsatisfactory' and 'inadequate', so it took several seconds to comprehend Mrs Rigby's news.

"Several of the apprentices have taken the opportunity to run away.

Utterly disgraceful behaviour, I'm sure... The only information we have is that unfortunately, your brother was involved and has been seriously hurt, although we will have to wait until my husband returns to hear the details."

A scream died in Keziah's throat, making a strangled sound.

"I am so sorry, Miss Bonner, I can see this has come as a great shock. There will, of course, be no lessons today, so if you'd like to return to your room, I'll send Mary to inform you when I know more."

Keziah stumbled out of the morning room and made her way upstairs in a daze.

*How selfish you are, worrying about yourself and about being dismissed, while all the time, Henry needed you.*

If he had been involved in the attack, he'd be found and arrested. How would he cope in the darkness and confinement of a gaol? And if he survived the filth and contagion, what if he was found guilty? Would he be hanged? Or transported like their sister?

Wild, maniacal laughter bubbled in her throat.

She'd been the cause of Eva's downfall and now she'd failed Henry. Her life was useless. Pointless.

Keziah surveyed the valley from her window seat, waiting for the return of the men and for more news. She pressed her palms to her temples. So many thoughts chased each other through her mind, she felt like her head might break open. If only there was something she could do to help find Henry, but she would only be in the way of the searches that had been going on for hours. Dogs baying and the occasional shout as the men systematically searched the woods let her know the hunt was continuing but if they didn't find Henry by nightfall, they would stop.

*Useless, useless, useless!*

She had been unable to keep Henry safe and could do nothing for him now. Could she have prevented this if she'd still worked in the mill? She couldn't have stopped him being influenced by Jack Lawley – she'd certainly tried but perhaps she could have persuaded him not to run away.

She'd told herself she had no choice but to go to Linderbourne Hall and take up the post of governess. But that simply hadn't been true. If she'd thanked Mrs Rigby for her offer and then turned her down, Keziah would have been at the mill when the trouble broke out and things might be different. But instead, although she'd known she had little chance of success, she'd stubbornly gone ahead anyway.

It was as if she'd begun to blur the distinction between real life and what might happen in the Other Place where the impossible seemed feasible. Ever since Matthew had burst into the schoolroom and her life, everything had changed. He'd infuriated, intrigued and enchanted her by turns until she couldn't think straight. It was his fault filling her head with the foolish notion of his imaginary world but thankfully, she'd had enough sense in the end, to reject him.

This was the best course for her. If Henry was found, she wouldn't stop until she'd done everything she could for her brother. She would give up her life for him if necessary.

And that would make up for the pain of losing Matthew.

In time...

Mary returned several times during the day with news – not of Henry – but of more disruption in the Hall. Matthew had departed for London early that morning in Mr Rigby's carriage. He'd left a letter for his uncle but both Mr and Mrs Rigby were furious and the last time Mary had come to Keziah's room, she'd been in tears.

"The mistress keeps snarlin' and snappin' at me like a dog. And Master said 'e'd never trust his nephew again. It ain't right! It ain't my fault Mr Matthew's gone!" she complained, "Crept out like a thief in the night, he did. Apparently, they'd gone into partnership but I heard Master say that Mr Matthew only said that to get his debts paid. You'd do well to stay in yer room. I wish I could keep out of everyone's way."

Matthew had gone? Keziah was stunned. Had he left because she'd turned him down? Surely that wasn't possible. But if he'd promised his uncle he'd go into partnership with him, why had he gone to London? He'd had doubts about his plans... but to return to his former life? His uncle would disown him and eventually, he'd find himself in a debtor's prison. What had he been thinking? Well, obviously, he hadn't been thinking at all. It was the sort of foolish thing someone did when they were desperate. Could it possibly have been because of her rejection of his marriage proposal?

"You'll never guess what I overheard!" Mary said the next time she appeared in Keziah's room, "That oaf, Osgood, told Mr Rigby his niece, Miss Lucy, had been up to no good with his brother, Tom, and that Mr Matthew had killed 'im! What d'you think of that?"

"Utter nonsense!" said Keziah sharply.

"That's what Mr Rigby said, except he weren't so polite about it."

"Mr Rigby didn't believe it, did he?" How dreadful it would be for Lucy if her secret had been discovered after all Matthew's attempts to protect her.

"No, he didn't. Although there's been a bit o' talk about Tom Osgood. He disappeared a few days ago and 'is brother is as mad as anything about it."

"I expect he left of his own accord," Keziah said quickly, "After all, wouldn't you if you had to live with that bully, John Osgood?"

"Yes, since you put it like that, I s'pose he might," Mary conceded.

"Yes, I'm certain of it." How could Keziah tell her Matthew had found Tom a job in London with Lord Sparham and had lent him the money for the journey? Mary would wonder how she knew and she could hardly tell her the truth.

If she couldn't tell Mary, she certainly couldn't tell Mr or Mrs Rigby. How sad that it was simply one more piece of evidence to use against Matthew – and it was completely undeserved. He'd done something kind for Tom and she knew Lord Sparham had accordingly reduced the sum he owed Matthew as he considered he'd discharged part of his debt by taking on the carpenter.

But the case against Matthew was damning. She couldn't believe he'd deliberately deceived her, nor yet that he was so weak he hadn't been able to resist the lure of London. It was tempting to believe the worst – which is what his uncle and aunt had done. Mr Rigby knew all about his dissolute lifestyle, after all, hadn't he paid the bills for several years? And Matthew had admitted as much to her.

Yet, unlike Mr Rigby, Keziah knew there was more to Matthew than that. Hadn't he risked injury – perhaps death when he met Osgood? Having Tom Osgood in Linderbourne had been a threat and there were many ways Matthew could have got rid of him but he'd chosen to find him a good job in London. He'd tried to secure Henry employment as a footman with his uncle – a boy he'd never even met. He had kindness to spare for others.

Unhappily, it seemed he had no kindness for himself. The life he'd been leading in London was proof of that. And once again, she wondered if he was resuming his path of self-destruction because of her. And yet, she'd had no choice.

But, in putting Henry first, had she hurt Matthew?

No, she told herself, it was conceited to imagine she'd been the cause of Matthew's flight. But if not her, then what? It was more proof – should any be needed that she knew very little about Matthew. Very little at all.

# Chapter Seven

Keziah leaned over the parapet of the bridge and stared into the depths of the Linderbourne River. Behind her, the giant waterwheel creaked as it turned, driven by the fast-flowing waters that gushed beneath her and then rushed onwards along the valley. And then, who knew where they went?

It had been over a week since Henry's disappearance. Despite rumours that had begun to circulate immediately that Henry had been the culprit, he had actually been the victim. Mr Rigby's investigations had revealed that it had started when John Osgood had accused Jack Lawley of failing to clean a loom. On seeing Osgood's cudgel, Jack had panicked and blamed Henry who'd protested his innocence. But Osgood seized Henry and set about teaching him a lesson.

To Jack's credit, he'd managed to wrestle the club from the overlooker's hand during his vicious attack on Henry and had lashed out wildly, catching Osgood on the side of the head.

Everyone realised the seriousness of the situation when Osgood collapsed. After a few seconds of stunned silence, panic ensued and fearing punishment, the apprentices fled, although they'd all been rounded up relatively quickly.

All except Henry. Despite his injuries which by all accounts were severe, he'd never been found and Keziah wondered if he'd stumbled out of the mill, into the river and been washed away. Was his body now miles downriver?

Staring down into the gushing water, she wondered yet again, why of all her family, had she survived?

Unlike her, their lives had all been of some importance.

Their mother had given them the most precious gift of life. While he'd been alive, their father had provided for them all. Eva had given up her life for her brother and sister and now, it seemed Henry's death had also achieved something. Following his investigations, Mr Rigby had forbidden physical punishment in his mill. He'd been so appalled at what had happened, he'd pardoned all the apprentices who'd run away. Furthermore, working conditions had been improved, so, if only in Linderbourne, Henry's death had accomplished a great deal.

But what had she ever achieved?

Nothing.

If Eva was dead, it was because of her. And if Henry had died, she hadn't been the cause yet she'd been unable to save him.

Sadly, Keziah knew Henry had carried the guilt of his mother's death all his life. Mama had died several days after his birth and he'd always believed he'd been the cause. She'd tried to convince him otherwise but she knew he hadn't believed her. And he'd died with that guilt.

A few days after the search for Henry had been called off, Keziah had resumed her duties as the girls' governess. Everyone had been very kind to her including the girls who seemed to have grown fond of her. She'd retreated into herself and was going through the everyday motions of life without thought or feeling.

For the first time in her life, she wondered what it would be like to share her grief with someone. What a relief it would be to pour her heart out and to feel strong arms around her.

That, however, was unlikely to happen. She stared down into the dark, swirling depths and wondered how deep the water was.

"Isn't that Cousin Matthew getting out of the carriage?" Blanche asked. Immediately her two sisters were by her side, peering out of the schoolroom window.

"Return to your seats, please, girls. If you are needed, your mama will call for you," At the mention of Matthew's name, Keziah began to tremble and all authority went from her voice. Could it be true? Matthew had returned?

The girls took no notice of her.

"I'm sure Mama would want us to greet him," Blanche said and hurried from the room followed by Rose and Violet.

"Girls!"

But they'd gone.

Keziah had no option but to go after them. As she hurried along the hall to the staircase she could hear raised voices.

"So, the prodigal returns!" Mr Rigby's voice rang out and at the rare sound of such anger, his three daughters stopped abruptly at the top of the stairs. Since Keziah had been at the Hall, she'd heard him shout but he'd never raised his voice to this level.

Mrs Rigby pleaded with him to allow Matthew a chance to speak and Lucy joined in but Mr Rigby would not be stopped. "If you think I'll pay another penny of your debts, think again! It's not the money, it's the deceit! I trusted you and you repaid me by running back to your debauched ways. And now, you have the audacity to return!"

Keziah reached the girls. She placed her arms around their shoulders and was about to silently shepherd them back to the schoolroom in case their father should turn his wrath upon them when she heard Matthew's voice for the first time. She saw him in the hall below.

"I assure you, Uncle..." He swayed slightly and his voice was slurred.

"You are an utter disgrace, sir! Drunk at this hour! How dare you come to my home and upset the ladies!"

Matthew held up his hand and surprisingly, Mr Rigby was silent.

"I have come with news." Matthew's voice was strained as if making an effort to speak clearly. "Firstly, Lucy, I am sad to say, our father passed away a few days ago."

There was a gasp from Lucy. Aunt Hannah emitted a low wail, then dabbed her eyes with her handkerchief.

Mr Rigby put his arm around his wife and realising the importance of the news he cleared his throat, his anger subsiding. "I see, well, my boy, in that case, I would like to offer my condolences to you and Lucy." His tone suggested he wanted to add 'however' and then continue berating his nephew.

Matthew staggered again and Lucy ran to him and put her arm around him. He flinched and drew away. "I also have other news but first I wish to beg your indulgence and would ask for your pardon for the apprentices who ran away."

"Apprentices?" spluttered Mr Rigby. "What are you talking about, man? What drunken nonsense is this? I understand your grief at a time like this but what have my apprentices to do with—"

Matthew cut in, "There is an apprentice who I would like to work for me and I'm prepared to pay a good price to reimburse you."

"He's rambling, poor dear," wailed Mrs Rigby. "The grief has addled his brain."

Keziah frowned. Was this a drunken attempt to buy her? Surely not! She was no longer an apprentice, she was now an employee.

"Had you been here, where you should have been," Mr Rigby said coldly, "you would have known I pardoned all the apprentices. And you would know John Osgood has been dismissed. There have been many changes since you left but that is none of your business now since you made it clear where your interests lie."

"Then would you have any objection if I paid you for one particular person?"

Mr Rigby laughed. "And with what will you pay me, Matthew? My own money?"

Slowly and deliberately Matthew reached into his pocket and withdrew a bundle of money which he held out with a shaking hand to his uncle.

As he did so, Lucy gasped. "Matthew is that blood?"

Mrs Rigby screamed and would have swooned had Mr Rigby not had his arm around her and caught her.

"It is nothing. Merely a graze," Matthew looked down as if surprised at the spreading, red stain on his shirt and taking an unsteady step towards his uncle, he held out the money. "I wish to pay this so that I can take Henry Bonner as my footman." With that, he crumpled to the floor, banknotes fluttering around him.

A servant was despatched to bring the doctor and as Matthew was carried upstairs to his bedroom, Keziah heard him rambling about ships and travelling to Switzerland. She was frantic to know more but there was confusion everywhere and she led the subdued girls back to the schoolroom.

Lucy looked at her apologetically, sympathetic that mention of Henry would have brought back the pain of his loss. But Matthew had been in London. How would he have known what had happened?

Keziah and the three girls remained in the schoolroom and as no one dared to venture downstairs and risk upsetting Mr or Mrs Rigby further, Mary brought a meal up for them. She promised to bring news if she heard anything.

"The doctor said that wound was caused by a bullet and he suspects Mr Matthew – or I suppose I should say Sir Matthew, now his father's gone – God rest his soul – has been in a duel. Mr Rigby's beside himself with rage and he's questioning Taylor. He's Sir Matthew's footman," she added when she saw Keziah's puzzled expression.

"Mrs Rigby, poor lady, has been sobbing since Sir Matthew arrived. I suppose the death of her brother must have come as a shock. Miss Lucy is sitting with Sir Matthew waiting for him to wake up but apparently, he's still delirious and talking all manner o' nonsense. But he keeps asking for you, miss," she said to Keziah. "So, Miss Lucy wondered if you'd be good enough to join her."

"Carry on with your reading, girls," Keziah said, following Mary to Matthew's room.

The curtains were drawn and it was dark and stuffy in the bedroom. The doctor was arranging his blood-letting bowls on the table next to Matthew who lay in the huge bed, his face flushed and beaded with sweat.

"He really ought not to have undertaken such a long journey," the doctor said to Lucy, shaking his head. "The infection has had a chance to take hold. Now only time will tell."

Matthew's head turned from side to side and his mouth moved as he mumbled meaningless sentences. Suddenly, his eyes opened and he seemed to focus on Keziah. He extended his fingers towards her. "Henry is safe..." His voice was cracked and faint, "I wanted you to know. And you and Henry will..." but he didn't have the strength to finish the sentence.

Lucy looked at Keziah in horror and mouthed, I'm so sorry.

Keziah took over the nursing and Lucy returned shortly after, her eyes shining and an enormous smile lighting her face.

"Keziah, you simply won't believe it but it's true! Your brother is in London, as Matthew said. He really is alive. Uncle is questioning Taylor and he confirmed it." Lucy threw her arm around Keziah's shoulders and held her until the sobs of relief subsided.

"How?" Keziah finally asked.

"Taylor said that minutes after leaving Linderbourne Hall, early on the morning of Osgood's attack, Matthew's coach driver spotted Henry lying in the middle of the road leading from the village. When the coach stopped, Henry came around sufficiently to explain he'd run away and Matthew decided to find medical help at their first night's stop, rather than delay his journey back to London and risk Henry being arrested."

So, Henry had been coming to find her. That seemed a likely explanation. The other apprentices had hidden in the woods. Henry had wanted to find her but he'd been too injured to make it to the Hall.

"Why didn't he write and tell me where he was?" Keziah asked.

"I believe," Lucy said slowly, "Henry was quite ill. Matthew engaged an eminent physician and he prescribed complete rest until the bruising had healed..." she paused and after biting her lower lip, she continued. "I must warn you, Henry was badly hurt and he... he may not walk again. But Taylor said the last time he saw Henry, a few days ago, the swelling was going down. I'm so sorry, my dear. As to why no one wrote, I'm afraid I can only imagine that they thought Henry might be arrested."

Lucy rotated the ring on her finger nervously. Finally, she said, "I'm so sorry, I realise this is not a good time but I have a favour to ask of you, Keziah. My uncle and aunt have decided to leave for London today so they can attend the funeral. Of course, I want to go with them but I can't bear the idea of leaving Matthew while he's so ill... unless I know you're looking after him for me. I can see you care for him and I would trust no one else. No! Don't try to deny it," she wagged her finger at Keziah, "I know my brother well and I could see he cared about you deeply. Why he rushed away to London, I have no notion but even now, I can see the love in your eyes. Perhaps we could look after each other's brothers?" Her eyes were pleading. "You could nurse Matthew and I'll bring Henry back to you."

Several hours later, Mr and Mrs Rigby, their three daughters and a reluctant Lucy set off for London in their carriage. She'd almost refused to go as Matthew was still delirious but she'd finally been persuaded when she'd learnt Dr Frobisher had agreed to call again later that day.

The Hall was silent once they'd gone. Keziah sat next to Matthew's bed in the dark, stuffy room, dampening his parched lips and dabbing his brow with a cool, damp cloth.

She paused, believing she heard him call her name but as she listened intently, she realised he was merely rambling, his head moving from side to side. His brow furrowed as if he was arguing with someone and periodically, she thought she heard him call his father.

Keziah longed to open the window and breathe fresh air but Dr Frobisher had forbidden it, insisting on a dark, hot room. She cooled Matthew's brow again and realised that other than encounters in the Hall such as passing him on the stairs, mostly, she'd been with him in the dark. Moving the lamp closer, she studied his face. If the worst should happen, she wanted to remember every detail. How handsome he was. It brought a lump to her throat to think this man had said he loved and wanted her. Of course, that was only within the safety of their imaginations in the Other Place. And she had fallen in love with him too.

But now, as she considered he might not survive this infection, she acknowledged it wouldn't matter where she was, she loved him completely. Not that it would make a difference to her life. It would be part of her she would carry forever and no one would ever know – especially not Matthew.

"Fool!" Keziah whispered. He had so much to offer life and yet he was intent on throwing it all away. He'd been duelling and had undoubtedly spent time gambling – where else would he have acquired that large sum of money he'd tried to give to his uncle – and that probably meant drinking to excess too. She squeezed her eyes tightly shut as if trying to banish the thought of the women who might have accompanied him. His promise to change had been hollow.

That's unfair, she told herself. Would he have gone to London if she'd accepted his proposal?

She didn't know, but she'd endured enough guilt during her life, she couldn't bear to shoulder any more. In the end, Matthew had made his own decisions, as had Henry. She'd tried her best to influence her brother and had failed. Eva had tried her best to influence Keziah and she'd also failed. Had their parents lived longer, would they have tried to control their three children and have failed?

And it wasn't just her family. Sir Hugh had withheld his love from Matthew simply because in his estimation, he didn't live up to his brother. He'd forbidden his sister to marry the man she loved and despite her wishes to the contrary, he'd fought a duel to uphold her honour. How different would the lives of all the Gregory family members have been if Sir Hugh had loved them all unconditionally and allowed them to make their own mistakes? How different would her life have been if she hadn't felt she had to control Henry's life?

For the first time, she saw that what she thought was best, might not be what Henry wanted – or indeed – needed. She'd become so used to trying to guide him, she'd lost sight of the fact he'd soon be a man and would want to make his own decisions.

Had Sir Hugh merely wanted to control his family or did he truly believe he knew best? And how about her? She'd always thought she'd had the best intentions for her family. But, had she simply wanted to be in control?

When Henry came back to Linderbourne, she would ensure he was well cared for but allow him to make his own decisions. She wouldn't try to force him to do anything. For the first time ever, she felt a weight lift from her. Of course, there would be nothing she could do to make anything up to Eva, it was too late for that.

"No! Father!" Matthew shouted and throwing his head from side to side, he reached out with one hand, only to let it drop back to the bed and then to mutter incoherently. She cooled his brow again and spoke soothingly to him.

He appeared to be reliving an argument with Sir Hugh. Taylor had told Mr Rigby that during a prolonged argument between Matthew and his father, he'd overheard Sir Hugh threaten to cut Matthew out of his will. However, he'd died later that evening and it was unlikely he'd had time to carry out his threat.

Mary had offered to take over from Keziah but she'd wanted to be there while the fever raged. He muttered again and reached out his hand but he was so weak, it fell back to the bed. Curling her fingers over his, she saw his expression soften as he seemed to calm and she experienced a rush of love. And why not? They were alone and therefore, no one would know.

She dozed and when she awoke, she realised the hand beneath hers was cooler and his face less flushed. For a horrifying second, she wondered if he'd passed away while she'd slept, but his breathing which had been laboured and ragged was now deep and regular. As she touched his chest to make sure, his eyes opened and he slowly looked around the room. When he focused on her, he smiled weakly.

"I had the strangest dream," he whispered, frowning as if trying to remember. "It's hard to untangle it from reality."

"Hush!" she said, pushing his damp fringe out of his eyes. "You've been so ill... and I've been so afraid..."

She helped him to take a sip of water and he sank back gratefully into the pillows.

"I must speak with my uncle." He frowned anxiously.

"He's at your father's funeral. You were too ill to join them. I'm so sorry."

"No matter. Father wouldn't care. And I wanted to tell you about Henry. I knew you'd be distraught. At first, I thought he might die. There seemed no kindness in telling you he'd been rescued only for you to learn he hadn't survived. He begged me not to tell you in case he was arrested. He said if we let you know you'd find some way of coming to London and then he'd probably be found." He relaxed back into the pillows and closed his eyes as if exhausted.

Keziah hung her head. How well Henry had known her. She wouldn't have listened if he'd asked her to stay away, once again assuming she knew best. Why did she never listen?

"Keziah," Matthew's voice was faint but insistent. "I need to tell you. In case I die, you must know..."

"Hush! You're still so weak. Wait until you're stronger."

"No, I can't rest until you know." He gripped her hand as tightly as he could and although she could have easily slipped his grasp, she allowed him to hold her and to continue.

"I know everyone believes I went back to London to carry on my old life but it's not true. I had to see my lawyer."

"Because your father threatened to cut you from his will?"

"Will?" His brows drew together as if he was trying to pin down his thoughts. "Oh, no, not that. I engaged a lawyer some time ago about a different matter."

Keziah wondered if his mind was still wandering.

He clutched her hand, "The duel, I need to tell you about the duel. It wasn't because of some jealous husband as I suppose Uncle assumed..." He struggled for breath and she urged him to stop and rest but he was determined to continue.

"The duel took place as a result of my findings. I want you to know. And the money. I admit it came from gambling but it was what Lord Sparham owed me. I swear I didn't place one wager while I was in

London, and I was sober the whole time – I had to keep a clear head. A clear head..." His voice tailed off. He closed his eyes and his chest heaved at the effort of speaking.

"Pray stop. You can explain further when you're recovered." She was desperate for his words to be true. If at some stage in the future she discovered he'd lied she knew she'd never trust anyone again. But was he in his right mind? Perhaps he was describing a dream. Was he aware of the difference between truth and lies?

He swallowed and started again. "I'll rest when you know everything..." He held her hand tightly again. "My lawyer searched for information about your father's watchmakers' shop and discovered his partner George Youngson had set up a business in Switzerland, on the proceeds of what he'd stolen."

George Youngson. How she hated that name. And he'd been living on her father's hard-earned money in Switzerland?

"The morning I left, I'd received a letter to say Youngson had returned to England and that's why I rushed away. I left a note for my uncle telling him I'd be back but I can understand why, with my reputation, he didn't believe it. Of course, I didn't mention my real reason for going to London. I didn't want to implicate you."

"But why? What did you hope to achieve?"

"Justice. I wanted justice for you and Henry. I confronted Youngson and demanded the money he'd stolen be returned to you, with interest, or I'd inform the authorities."

Keziah gasped. "What did he say?"

"He denied it but I persisted. Then, he challenged me to a duel."

"You fought a duel because of me?" She looked at him in horror. How could she have once believed he'd put himself in danger on a whim? He could have died trying to get justice for her and Henry.

Matthew nodded wearily. "He grazed my arm. I put a bullet in his leg. Nothing fatal, but it appeared to make him feel his honour had been restored. He agreed to pay you compensation. All... for you... and Henry." He lay back, exhausted. But for the first time, his face was at peace.

Dr Frobisher was pleased with Matthew's progress, pronouncing him out of danger.

"I dare say by the time Mr Rigby returns from London, Sir Matthew will be well on the mend."

Keziah longed for the family's return because it would mean she'd once again see Henry, yet she dreaded it too. If the doctor was correct, Matthew would be well enough to no longer need nursing and as soon as he was well, he'd take Henry with him to London where he'd train as a footman. As the new baronet, Matthew would need to find a wife and if his uncle could be persuaded to resume their partnership, then he would be busy planning a new mill and village.

Neither Henry nor Matthew would need her. And now, George Youngson had paid her compensation, she had sufficient to live independently. When Matthew told her Youngson had paid a sum of money, she'd expected a small sum. Perhaps enough to live quietly. But Matthew's lawyer had negotiated a very large sum of money. Youngson had obviously invested her father's money well and now much of it had found its way back to the Bonner children. Well, two of them at any rate.

It was time to take control of her own life. She'd see Mrs Rigby when she returned to Linderbourne Hall and suggest Miss Maynard would be perfect to take over her post. Then, she would leave for London and find a job teaching workhouse children in a charity school like Mr Dawley who'd taught her all those years ago. At least she'd be able to do something useful for them while they were in her charge.

At long last, she'd be free to do as she chose but the elation she thought she'd feel, was strangely lacking and she wondered why she wasn't happier. Of course, her dream had now changed because it wouldn't include Henry unless that was what he wanted, and if he didn't, a lonely future stretched ahead of her.

"You seem troubled..." Matthew's brow furrowed as he regarded her. "I thought you'd be happy."

"Yes, I am." She tried to sound convincing. "It's hard to take so much in and to imagine what changes will need to be made."

"Ah, changes. Yes. Happy ones for you but perhaps not so much for me..." He sighed.

"But now you're the baronet, you can do whatever you like."

"My father has left many debts. I have two options and one of those will probably be denied me. I can either marry a rich woman or try to persuade my uncle I can be trusted as his business partner. But if I can't..."

"Then you must marry a rich woman." She forced her mouth to form the words and once they'd been spoken, she'd dreaded his reply.

Don't be so selfish, she told herself, if that is what he wants then that is what must happen. She had an income and had therefore moved up in society. He'd also moved up now he was a baronet and so, the gulf between them had simply moved and widened.

"I have an heiress in mind," he said with a frown. "But I feel she'll take some winning over before she accepts me."

Keziah tried to swallow the lump in her throat. She couldn't bear to hear more of this woman.

"You haven't asked who the lady is..." he said his eyes narrowed, as he observed her.

She shook her head unable to speak but finally managed, "I can't bear to know."

"May I assume that is because you care?"

Well, what did it matter if she admitted the truth? And after all, he'd been honest with her.

"Yes... I wasn't truthful when I told you I didn't care."

"Then why did you tell me that...?" He stared at her in disbelief. "What possible reason could you have had?"

"Because we could never have been together and I thought it kinder if you believed I didn't care."

"But we can be together."

"No! Not in real life. The Other Place doesn't exist, Matthew! Please don't make this harder."

"Then, let me ask you this, do you love me, like I love you?"

She nodded, regarding him sadly.

"Then we will make it work."

How tempting it was to believe him but she knew it wasn't possible. Unless... Perhaps he wasn't thinking of the Other Place, perhaps he was no longer proposing marriage. After all, many men married wealthy women and then kept a mistress. Is that what he meant? And if so, how did she feel about that prospect? Would she be able to share him with another woman? The alternative was to lose him completely.

He reached out and took her hand. Had he misinterpreted the silence while she tried to untangle her thoughts, as agreement to be his mistress?

"You know I would always look after you?" He raised his eyebrows in question. "But perhaps, like the rest of the family, you don't trust me?"

She stared at him in silence, still trying to imagine what life might be like if she agreed.

He shook his head sadly, "I know it's my own fault but I thought, somehow, you had seen the real me."

"I do trust you, Matthew," she said quickly. "I just never saw myself as any man's mistress. I need to think."

"Mistress? Is that what you think I'm proposing?" he looked at her in horror, "Keziah, I want you to be my wife!"

"But you said you need a rich wife. You said you had someone in mind."

"And I do. It's you."

"I know I have some money from George Youngson but I'm hardly an heiress."

"I'm not interested in anyone's fortune. I'm determined to win the trust of my uncle and if I fail, then I will set up in business with someone else or on my own. Somehow, I will secure the Gregory townhouse and estates and I'll be able to settle a large sum on Lucy for her marriage. There will be many in my social circle who will ostracise me and so, although I've inherited a baronetcy, I will no longer belong to my class and that means that as a woman who has her own income, you and I are not so far apart and in fact, I'd say we were perfectly suited. So, Mistress Keziah Bonner, will you do me the honour of becoming my wife?"

# CHAPTER EIGHT

The Gregory carriage jolted as it went down a rut and Henry winced. Osgood's attack had left him with serious injuries but over the last few years, he'd regained the use of his leg although he knew he'd always limp. He cast his mind back to his first journey from London to Linderbourne so many years ago in that uncomfortable straw-lined cart. Keziah had cradled his head in her lap when he felt sick at the jerking motion although he'd known she felt just as nauseous as he. Henry looked across at her now. She was holding hands with his brother-in-law, Sir Matthew Gregory. It hardly seemed possible she'd now found happiness.

Henry had been surprised there hadn't been more resistance from Mr Rigby despite the substantial amount of money that had been returned to the Bonner family from the man Henry didn't remember, but who'd callously thrust him and his sisters into poverty. And yet, Mr Rigby had been delighted and had given Keziah away at the wedding.

His wonderful, loving sister. For so long, he'd carried the guilt of his mother's death but as Keziah had often told him, and he now knew to be true, it hadn't been his fault. As a newborn, he'd had no intention of causing harm. Unlike George Youngson, who'd deliberately defrauded his partner's family. And with the freedom from his guilt, he knew that his sister had put aside hers. Knowing her as he did, he expected there was still some residual guilt but, in a few days, he hoped she would be able to put it all behind her. For they were on their way to London for the return of the Royal Seraph, which had set sail from Sydney, many months before. On board the ship was his sister, Eva, and her husband.

Against all odds, while Matthew's lawyer had investigating George Youngson, he'd discovered one of his colleagues had been trying to find Keziah and Henry on behalf of Eva's husband. They'd both remarked on the coincidence of working on cases involving such an unusual surname as Bonner and had compared notes. And now the Bonner children – all grown up – would be reunited. The thought made him swallow back tears of joy. How wonderful that his two sisters had both found good men who'd been of a common mind to bring the family together again.

Henry was still young but one day in the not too distant future, he would marry too. He looked at the girl sitting next to Keziah and smiled at her. Mary flushed and smiled shyly back. Once a serving girl in Linderbourne Hall, she was now Keziah's lady's maid. He'd had plenty of time to get to know her at Linderbourne Hall when he'd been convalescing and they'd compared stories about working in the mill and having experienced a traumatic incident that had left them both with physical and mental scars. They shared a special bond and one day, he would make it official and then at last the three Bonner children would have found love and peace.

Henry's eyes flicked to Keziah and saw she'd intercepted the smile and he knew his sister approved of his attachment to Mary. How well she knew him and how much he owed her. She raised her eyebrows slightly and with a smile, he touched the tip of his nose and returning his smile, she did the same. Everything was well.

\* \* \*

If you enjoyed this story, please consider leaving a review on Amazon mybook.to/TheDuchessOfSydney. For information about other books in this series, please go to https://dawnknox.com and sign up for the newsletter. Thank you.

# About the Author

Dawn spent much of her childhood making up stories filled with romance, drama and excitement. She loved fairy tales, although if she cast herself as a character, she'd more likely have played the part of the Court Jester than the Princess. She didn't recognise it at the time, but she was searching for the emotional depth in the stories she read. It wasn't enough to be told the Prince loved the Princess, she wanted to know how he felt and to see him declare his love. She wanted to see the wedding. And so, she'd furnish her stories with those details.

Nowadays, she hopes to write books that will engage readers' passions. From poignant stories set during the First World War to the zany antics of the inhabitants of the fictitious town of Basilwade; and from historical romances, to the fantasy adventures of a group of anthropomorphic animals led by a chicken with delusions of grandeur, she explores the richness and depth of human emotion.

A book by Dawn will offer laughter or tears – or anything in between, but if she touches your soul, she'll consider her job well done.

You can follow her here on https://dawnknox.com
Amazon Author Central: mybook.to/DawnKnox
on Facebook: https://www.facebook.com/DawnKnoxWriter
on Twitter: https://twitter.com/SunriseCalls
on Instagram: https://www.instagram.com/sunrisecalls/
on YouTube: shorturl.at/luDNQ

# The Duchess of Sydney

The Lady Amelia Saga – Book One

Betrayed by her family and convicted of a crime she did not commit, Georgiana is sent halfway around the world to the penal colony of Sydney, New South Wales. Aboard the transport ship, the Lady Amelia, Lieutenant Francis Brooks, the ship's agent becomes her protector, taking her as his "sea-wife" – not because he has any interest in her but because he has been tasked with the duty.

Despite their mutual distrust, the attraction between them grows. But life has not played fair with Georgiana. She is bound by family secrets and lies. Will she ever be free again – free to be herself and free to love?

Order from Amazon: mybook.to/TheDuchessOfSydney
Paperback: ISBN: 9798814373588
eBook: ASIN: B09Z8LN4G9

# The Finding of Eden

The Lady Amelia Saga – Book Two

1782 – the final year of the Bonner family's good fortune. Eva, the eldest child of a respectable London watchmaker becomes guardian to her sister, Keziah, and brother, Henry. Barely more than a child herself, she tries to steer a course through a side of London she hadn't known existed. But her attempts are not enough to keep the family together and she is wrongfully accused of a crime she didn't commit and transported to the penal colony of Sydney, New South Wales on the Lady Amelia.

Treated as a virtual slave, she loses hope. Little wonder that when she meets Adam Trevelyan, a fellow convict, she refuses to believe they can find love.

Order from Amazon: mybook.to/TheFindingOfEden
Paperback: ISBN: 9798832880396
eBook: ASIN: B0B2WFD279

# THE OTHER PLACE

The Lady Amelia Saga – Book Three

1790 – the year Keziah Bonner and her younger brother, Henry, exchange one nightmare for another. If only she'd listened to her elder sister, Eva, the Bonner children might well have remained together. But headstrong Keziah had ignored her sister's pleas. Eva had been transported to the far side of the world for a crime she hadn't committed and Keziah and Henry had been sent to a London workhouse. When the prospect of work and a home in the countryside is on offer, both Keziah and Henry leap at the chance. But they soon discover they've exchanged the hardship of the workhouse for worse conditions in the cotton mill.

The charismatic but irresponsible nephew of the mill owner shows his interest in Keziah. But Matthew Gregory's attempts to demonstrate his feelings – however well-intentioned – invariably results in trouble for Keziah. Is Matthew yet another of Keziah's poor choices or will he be a major triumph?

Order from Amazon:
Paperback: ISBN
eBook: ASIN

# THE DOLPHIN'S KISS

The Lady Amelia Saga – Book Four

Born 1790; in Sydney, New South Wales, to wealthy parents, Abigail Moran is attractive and intelligent, and other than a birthmark on her hand that her mother loathes, she has everything she could desire. Soon, she'll marry handsome, witty, Hugh Hanville. Abigail's life is perfect. Or is it?
A chance meeting with a shopgirl, Lottie Jackson, sets in motion a chain of events that finds Abigail in the remote reaches of the Hawkesbury River with sea captain, Christopher Randall. He has inadvertently stumbled across the secret that binds Abigail and Lottie. Will he be able to help Abigail come to terms with the secret or will Fate keep them apart?

Order from Amazon:
Paperback: ISBN eBook: ASIN

# The Great War

100 Stories of 100 Words Honouring Those Who Lived And Died 100 Years Ago

One hundred short stories of ordinary men and women caught up in the extraordinary events of the Great War – a time of bloodshed, horror and heartache. One hundred stories, each told in exactly one hundred words, written one hundred years after they might have taken place. Life between the years of 1914 and 1918 presented a challenge for those fighting on the Front, as well as for those who were left at home—regardless of where that home might have been. These stories are an attempt to glimpse into the world of everyday people who were dealing with tragedies and life-changing events on such a scale that it was unprecedented in human history. In many of the stories, there is no mention of nationality, in a deliberate attempt to blur the lines between winners and losers, and to focus on the shared tragedies. This is a tribute to those who endured the Great War and its legacy, as well as a wish that future generations will forge such strong links of friendship that mankind will never again embark on such a destructive journey and will commit to peace between all nations.

*"This is a book which everyone should read - the pure emotion which is portrayed in each and every story brings the whole of their experiences - whether at the front or at home - incredibly to life. Some stories moved me to tears with their simplicity, faith and sheer human endeavour." (Amazon)*

Order from Amazon: mybook.to/TheGreatWar100

Paperback: ISBN 978-1532961595
eBook: ASIN B01FFRN7FW
Hardcover: ISBN 979-8413029800

# THE FUTURE BROKERS
**Written as DN Knox with Colin Payn**

It's 2050 and George Williams considers himself a lucky man. It's a year since he—like millions of others—was forced out of his job by Artificial Intelligence. And a year since his near-fatal accident. But now, George's prospects are on the way up. With a state-of-the-art prosthetic arm and his sight restored, he's head-hunted to join a secret Government department—George cannot believe his luck.

He is right not to believe it. George's attraction to his beautiful boss, Serena, falters when he discovers her role in his sudden good fortune, and her intention to exploit the newly-acquired abilities he'd feared were the start of a mental breakdown.

But, it turns out both George and Serena are being twitched by a greater puppet master and ultimately, they must decide whose side they're on—those who want to combat Climate-Armageddon or the powerful leaders of the human race.

Order from Amazon: <u>mybook.to/TheFutureBrokers</u>
Paperback: ISBN 979-8723077676
eBook: ASIN B08Z9QYH5F

Printed in Great Britain
by Amazon

21015569R00078